RAIN GIRL

WITHDRAWN

RAIN GIRL

GABI KRESLEHNER
Translated by Lee Chadeayne

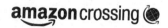

Rain Girl was first published in 2010 by Ullstein Buchverlage GmbH, Berlin, as *Das Regenmädchen*. Translated from German by Lee Chadeayne. First published in English by AmazonCrossing in 2014.

Published by AmazonCrossing, Seattle
www.apub.com

Amazon, the Amazon logo, and AmazonCrossing are trademarks of Amazon.com, Inc., or its affiliates.

ISBN-13: 9781477823118
ISBN-10: 1477823115

Library of Congress Control Number: 2013923378

Cover design by Lindsay Heider Diamond

Printed in the United States of America

1

She staggered along the northbound shoulder of the autobahn in the mist of the rising dawn unaware of the danger hurtling toward her. She was blind to the harsh light reflecting on her dress, making it glitter and sparkle one last time before being swallowed up by the dirt and the rain.

She screamed when she was sent flying through the air—into the open sky—but no one heard her on the A9 just outside Munich on the morning she would not live to see. As if she were waking up on any normal day, her body rolled over. Her eyes were wide open, staring into the sky.

By the time the car finished lurching wildly back and forth and screeched to a stop, she was dead—killed pursuing her dreams on her way to Berlin.

Help came too late for the girl lying in the middle of the road—her name not yet known, she was just a ghost in the drizzling rain, broken and still.

2

He was bent over, leaning against his BMW, his heart racing. He felt like he was going to throw up—like he was going to spit out what had happened—but at the same time he knew he couldn't. Knew that this would stay with him for the rest of his life.

His entire body shook, and he wished he were back in his girlfriend's cozy apartment, dreaming in her comforting arms. He didn't belong here—not on this morning, not in this shaking body, not on this autobahn toward Berlin.

She had appeared so suddenly. For a fraction of a second, he had seen her eyes and her mouth opened to scream. The impact was muffled, yet loud enough to resonate in his ears forever after. She had flown across the car and yards into the air—her body strangely weightless, like a rag doll.

He'd tried to get control of his car, stop its careening from side to side, and he didn't see where she landed.

Music was booming through his open car door as Aida and Radamès sang their swan song—one last bit of familiarity linking him to his former life.

Suddenly the music stopped and someone was shaking him by the shoulders.

"Get ahold of yourself, man!"

He looked up to see someone standing beside him, looking at him intently. "What happened?"

He began to shake his head, slowly, in a daze. "I don't know," he said. "I don't know. All of a sudden she was there, out of nowhere, like a ghost."

The man shook his head and left.

Out of nowhere—yes, that's how it happened, out of nowhere, like a ghost. He suspected he would be saying that often from now on. Out of nowhere, like a ghost.

Slowly he began moving, climbing back into the car, closing the door carefully behind him, and restarting the opera. *Aida*, he thought, *sing for me; sing me back into my old life.* He closed his eyes and leaned back against the headrest. Gradually, calm came over him.

3

They did it once more standing up before she switched her cell phone back on. They didn't need words, never had. When they were together it was thorough and precise. Silence was their bed, silence the only soft and gentle part of it—nothing else.

Afterward she said, "Your back tastes like Portugal." He laughed.

"Yes," she said, "like Portugal, salt, the Atlantic. Laugh all you want."

"I know," he said, laughing. "Tides, wind, sun. You always say that."

They didn't talk in the bathroom. He watched her as she showered, though he knew she couldn't stand it.

Then her cell phone rang. He handed it to her as she turned the water off. It was Felix and he sounded excited. Probably annoyed.

"Jesus, Franza, finally! Why can't I reach you? What the hell are you doing? I've been calling you for half an hour! A body was found on the A9. When are you coming in? It's nine thirty!"

She nodded but didn't feel bad that she was late. "Yes," she said, but was thinking *what's fifteen minutes*? "All right, calm down, I'm coming. Twenty minutes. Are you going to wait for me?"

She'd needed a break—suddenly, urgently—a break from death, from dirt, from all that crap, and what was wrong with that? So instead of driving straight to work she'd switched off her cell phone at the red light and turned onto the road past the theater—toward him, toward Port.

She heard Felix sigh. "Twenty minutes! Where the hell are you?"

"Yes," she said, "twenty minutes. Exactly." She hung up, ignoring the rest of his question.

A body on the autobahn. Sounded like an accident. Why were she and Felix involved? They were homicide detectives.

She turned the water on again. It was cold. It ran over her face, and her teeth began to chatter. So out there in the spring rain that was supposed to make things grow there was a dead body.

She sighed. Apparently no accident then, or at least a suspicious one. The usual questions came to her: Who was it? What happened? How? And why?

"Do you have to go?" Port asked. "Too bad. I thought we'd have breakfast together."

Franza shook her head and got out of the shower. "Would you give me a minute, please?"

· · ·

He was leaning against the dining-room table with a dog-eared script in his hand. There was a shadow in his eyes, a hint of mockery.

For a moment she touched the crook of his neck, held her nose to his chest, and breathed in his smell. His lips tickled her ear as he recited a passage from the play he would soon star in.

Outside, the rain smelled of the approaching summer, and she stopped to enjoy its fragrance. She remembered something they used to say as children when walking in the rain: *Make me grow. Make me grow.*

That's what she had believed as a child, and even as a teenager. Rain in June makes things grow. It makes everything better, and it is as soft as velvet.

There weren't many things she still believed in. She had seen too much in her life, with her job. But the magic of rain in June had remained, and she ran out into the raindrops whenever she could—when it wasn't too embarrassing. She would stand with her eyes closed, face and arms toward the sky, hoping everything would be good and soft, and that everything would grow.

Port was a bit like rain in June year-round. He made everything easier to bear, even the coming heat of summer and the dead bodies, which would look sweaty and tired.

Ever since Franza had become a police detective she'd longed for the cold. When the snow crunched and the ice glittered in the sun, the dead looked different. Not as dead. More solemn. Better.

. . .

Felix Herz was standing outside the police station. "A girl," he said as he jumped into the car. "At first it looked like suicide. According to the driver of the car that hit her, she just appeared all of a sudden out of nowhere. But then things get mysterious: they found blood."

Franza frowned. "Blood? How is that mysterious? That's what you expect in a car accident."

"True," Felix said, "next to the body and around it. But not a hundred yards away in a rest area."

"Oh," Franza said, thinking it over for a moment. "But it's been raining for hours. Everything would have washed away."

"Right again," Felix said, "but not underneath a shelter." He paused and grinned. "Water usually comes from above, not below."

She was grinning, too. "We're onto something," she said.

Almost all of their work was in the field. Their jobs were hard. There were more and more dead bodies: the man who shot his wife and child, the junkie in the dumpster full of slaughtered pigs. The girl on the autobahn.

4

Ben saw Marie on the side of the road, noticed her nice tits. He zoomed past at a hundred miles an hour, the road a blur.

5

They had covered her with a tarp to protect her from the rain and the prying eyes of passing drivers, who were slowly being directed past the accident scene.

She was so young, too young to die, and she had a tenderness about her—the tenderness of the dead who were still between worlds, neither here nor there. The newly dead were still able to communicate what Franza needed to know to tell their stories. If she didn't listen, who would?

In two days' time the girl would be completely transformed: anything still linking her to this world would fall away, and she would be as clear and straight as never before, and truly gone. By then, everything in the girl's life would have passed on to Franza.

Felix didn't understand, he thought her introspection was a waste of time. But he always let her have those moments, left her the time to ask what had happened, even if the dead weren't answering yet. They just lay there, twisted or straight, dirty or clean, but always taken by death, always silent.

"Prepare yourself," Felix had said, "she's young."

But she was never sufficiently prepared. Franza shook her head, no, never enough, and she held back a sob.

I can't do it anymore, she thought. *I can't do it anymore. I'm too old. I need a different job.*

That was what she always thought before examining a body, before looking into its eyes and receiving its messages—and then she stayed, and investigated, and solved. It was like an addiction. Or a mission.

The girl was lying on a grassy strip alongside the road, small and skinny, a little bird fallen from the sky—and from life.

Rain had soaked her face, filled her still-open eyes—hazel eyes. They seemed to be staring into an endless space, understanding something that no one still living could know.

Her hair was a tangled mess of blood, rain, and dirt—impossible to tell the color, dark brown maybe, bordering on black. A strand lay across her face, dividing it into two halves. Franza kneeled next to the girl and carefully brushed the strand of hair to one side, putting the halves back together.

Sleep, Franza thought, *sleep. Rest, my darling.* She paused for a moment, looking down into the girl's open eyes before closing them.

Finally she got up and took a step back. The girl had no shoes on, no stockings, and her dress was pushed up on her thighs. It must have been a party dress, with its spangles and strings of pearls on silver fabric. It was like a precious gem that was no longer sparkling, smashed and soaked with blood and dirt—like its wearer.

"We don't have a name," Felix said. He had approached quietly and for the last few moments had been standing next to Franza. "She had no ID on her, no bag, no backpack, no cell phone—nothing."

"She's not much older than Ben," Franza said.

"I know," Felix said.

The sky was a muted blue, a halfhearted melody. The rain had ceased.

6

Marie on the side of the road, tits like honeydew melons.

"Hey, Ben!" she said, after he had turned around and pulled up beside her. "Can I get a ride?"

When Marie laughed with her mouth wide open, you could see a tiny moon, sparkling jewelry against her white teeth.

She asked whose car it was. "It's my dad's second car," he said. "But I can use it when he doesn't need it. And he pretty much never does since he has another." He grinned.

"Great!" she said. "That opens up the possibilities."

He shot her a sideways glance and struggled to keep the car on the road. "You think?" he asked.

"Yes," she said, "I think."

She turned away and looked out the window, smiling faintly, tapping her foot to the beat of the song that filled the car, leaving no room for anything else.

"Let's run away," she said finally, but too softly for him to hear. He turned the music down.

"What's that?"

"Run away!" she repeated. "Let's just take off! Anywhere. Somewhere where no one knows us, where we're strangers."

He was startled. He didn't like the idea at all, but didn't want to let it show—he liked her, and he wanted her to like him. So he just shrugged.

"I don't know," he said. "Are you serious?"

She turned to face him, still tapping to the beat. Her eyes were shining like freshly polished apples. "I want to take a bite out of you," she said. "I think you're sweet."

Her hand brushed down his arm to his knee, and he felt shivers running down his spine. His pants tightened. He pulled over to the side of the road.

Marie chuckled quietly. "Yes," she said, "very sweet indeed."

Then she kissed him. On the ear. It went BANG. She kissed him in the hollow just above his collarbone. Light as a breath of air.

"You are . . ." he whispered breathlessly, "I don't know."

She laughed quietly and he stopped talking. The tip of her tongue gently circled his eye. He was trembling. Just a little, but still.

7

"Tell me what happened," Franza said, trying to engage the man. He looked terrible—tired and pale, his tie loosened, and brown stains on his otherwise immaculate shirt.

An hour earlier when he was getting tired of waiting around a policeman had given him a cup of coffee from a thermos. It had been so hot he'd burned his lips and then spilled it, ruining his shirt.

Now this woman was standing in front of him, a homicide detective, and he couldn't understand why he had to repeat everything all over again, and why everything was taking so long. *It's just typical,* he thought angrily, *government workers! Regular salary, regular hours, all the comforts!*

He longed for his office, for his secretary, even for his wife—simply for something from his normal life.

It had taken forever for this detective lady—Franza Oberwieser, if he'd gotten the name right—and her partner to show up. What a strange name. They didn't even bother apologizing for keeping him waiting. Typical cops, did as they pleased and he had to pay for it.

"Listen," he said, his anger rising. "I've told this to you guys a million times now."

She gave him an understanding smile. "Yes," she said, "Herr Bohrmann, I know. But please tell me again anyway."

He took a deep breath. "All right," he sighed. "All right. I was on my way home, not really thinking of anything, listening to music, and then all of a sudden she was just there. Out of nowhere. Right in front of me, in less than a second—like a ghost. Believe me, there was nothing I could do. She just ran right out in front of my car. Just like that. Smack."

He fell silent, pain showing in his face. Franza prompted him. "And then? What happened then?"

He lifted his head and looked at her, pulling himself together.

"Then?" he asked quietly. "Nothing. I saw her eyes, just briefly. Almost not at all. It was raining. And she screamed, I think."

He fell silent again and looked down at his shoes.

"Where did she come from?" Franza asked.

He shrugged and pointed in various directions. "I don't know. From . . . somewhere. Maybe from somewhere back there. I think it might have been the rest area. Yes, that's right, the rest area. Where else could she have come from? From the fields? At night? I don't know."

Franza nodded. "Did you notice anything else?"

He shook his head. She could see he was confused and tired, but she kept asking questions anyway. She had to. First impressions were crucial.

"Is it possible she was being followed? Did you see anyone?"

"What? Followed? No idea!" He was startled, beginning to shake. "No! How should I know?"

"Calm down," Franza said. "Herr Bohrmann, just calm down. We're almost finished. Tell me if you saw anyone following her."

"No," he said, getting control of his voice and becoming calmer. "I didn't see anyone. Except for the man who called the police and ambulance and all that."

He pointed to the middle-aged man who was waving his hands around excitedly while being questioned by Felix. Franza glanced at the man and nodded.

"Listen," Bohrmann said, "are we finished yet? I'm dead tired and I've got work to do. My wife will be worried."

"Almost," the detective assured him. "Soon. One of my colleagues will take you home. Haven't you spoken to your wife yet?"

At that Bohrmann became suddenly nervous again. Franza raised her eyebrows with surprise and smiled to herself. It was always the same.

"Listen, I . . ." he stammered, "I haven't had a chance yet."

He swallowed, his anger rising again. "That's personal! It's none of your business!"

"Oh!" Franza said softly. "In this type of situation, everything is our business. You ran over a person, remember?" She wasn't surprised at the nasty tone in her voice, and thought briefly of Port.

He looked down at the ground, chewing on his lips.

"All right, then, let's forget about your wife. Back to you. Where were you coming from? What were you doing on the autobahn in the middle of the night?"

He didn't answer, just folded his arms on his chest and stared past her with hostility.

"Herr Bohrmann?"

She sensed his despair. *I'm sorry,* she thought, *but I can't do anything about it. You've fallen into my clutches now.*

He sighed, and it sounded like a sob. "All right," he said. "Shit. I was at . . . my girlfriend's, twenty miles south of here. As you can imagine, my wife doesn't know anything about it."

Franza whistled softly through her teeth. It really was always the same. "What did you tell your wife?"

He swallowed. "Weekend meeting in Hamburg. We just wanted a few days to ourselves for once, not just two or three hours like usual."

"Well," Franza said, "that really is tough luck. You'll have a few things to figure out."

The floodgates were now open, and he wanted to talk. He took Franza's hand, but she pulled it away.

"Listen, you've got to help me. She thinks I'm coming from Munich, from the airport. She's waiting at home. I was supposed to be back two hours ago."

Franza looked at him in disbelief. "Two hours ago? And you haven't called her yet? You just let her wait? She'll be worried! She's probably made a few phone calls and found out you weren't even on that plane!"

"She already tried calling me several times."

"And?"

"I didn't pick up." He looked at her helplessly. "What am I supposed to say?"

She shook her head and gave a little laugh. "You're asking me? How should I know? You should've thought of that before."

He became angry again. "How could I know this was going to happen? Shit like this only happens on TV!"

"You think?" Franza asked and thought of Port and his bizarre plan to sleep with the director of the next play to get the lead role. *That's* what usually happened only on TV.

"Tell her the truth," she said, and turned to leave.

He panicked, realizing that his world was collapsing. "I can't do that!" he said. "I just can't."

"The truth is always the best way out," she said, knowing it was complete bullshit.

She nodded to him and started to walk off, but then she turned around one more time. "You can leave now, by the way. My colleagues will take care of you. But keep yourself available in case we need you again."

He looked at her with drooping shoulders, lost for words. But then lifted his head high once more to have the last word. "Stupid bitch!" he yelled. "You can take the 'truth' and shove it!"

She didn't bother turning around. One of the officers would take care of him. Poor bastard. Wrong place, wrong time.

As she slowly made her way back to Felix, she thought of Port and the director of the play, whom she'd seen in a photo, and of Max and how he had become suspicious and thought it was Felix. Then the girl came back to her mind, her hazel eyes.

8

How the downy tufts of the dandelion seeds used to float through the air when they were children! Released in one puff, their white seeds rose, quivering and light, dancing into the sky. Marie squinted and sneezed again and again because she had looked into the sun for too long.

"You must have been crazy as a child," Ben said, holding a lavender stalk under her nose. It smelled wonderful, which didn't surprise her, and she knocked it out of his hand, stood up, and ascended to her heavenly kingdom.

What a weird dream, Ben thought in his dream. He felt his full bladder and woke up.

9

"So," Felix said, "what have we got so far?"

They were looking around the rest area about a hundred yards from the accident scene. The coroner, Dr. Borger, and the forensic team had finished their preliminary examination and were on their way back to the city. The girl had been placed gently into a gray metal coffin and taken away. Noon was approaching, and Franza was getting hungry.

The detectives were standing in front of a long wooden table with a bench on either side. There was a canopy overhead covered with shingles like an ordinary roof. On two sides it reached almost to the ground, offering protection from the weather. Beyond the table and benches but still underneath the roof, was a pile of large, jagged stones partially covered with moss. Ferns and low rosebushes covered with blossoms grew alongside.

Investigators had found traces of blood on the stones and assumed the blood belonged to the dead girl. Franza and Felix were sure the forensic examination in the lab would quickly confirm this, especially because under the table they had also found what they assumed was one of the girl's missing shoes—a high-heel shoe with straps decorated with rhinestones that matched the silver dress.

The ground around the table and benches was strewn with cigarette butts, broken glass, and other trash, which was not surprising considering how much traffic passed through here during the day, and as they were now discovering, during the night as well.

The forensic team took the shoe, trash, broken glass, and cigarette butts in as evidence. They would be examined for hours for any useful information, though you never knew in advance if they'd find anything. That's just the way it was. Like pieces of a puzzle slowly coming together, creating a picture.

Felix put his right foot on one of the benches, leaned his elbow on his knee, and thought out loud. "So, what have we got so far? Around five this morning, Tuesday, a disheveled girl stumbles onto the autobahn and gets hit and killed. It's possible she was drunk, but considering we found blood here, it's more likely she had been seriously injured before she was hit. She's wearing a party dress, and she's barefoot. We found one of her shoes here in the rest area."

They found a matching shoe near the accident scene, in front of the bushes in the grass next to the shoulder. The grass was trampled in places and matted down as if someone had been lying there for a while. There were also tire tracks. Someone must have been driving too fast and, failing to consider how slippery the wet road was, braked too hard and skidded off the shoulder into the grass.

The crime-scene investigators had erected a kind of tent to protect any evidence that hadn't been washed away yet, but the chances of getting a decent tire print were slim.

Felix pointed to the table and paused for a moment before continuing. "What's all this telling us?"

Franza shrugged. "That she was coming from a party, some special occasion—a birthday, graduation, christening, engagement, wedding . . . something like that."

"How did she get here?"

"Evidently not in her own vehicle, or we would have found it."

"So she was getting a ride with someone. Question is, who? And where to?"

"Anyway, she ended up here, at this rest area. Strange place."

They paused a moment. Then the Ping-Pong match resumed.

"Lovers?"

"Who else would stop at a rest area on the autobahn in the middle of the night?"

"Yeah, who else?" He scratched his chin. "But would you pick this place for a romantic encounter?"

She shrugged. "When you're really in love, who knows. On the other hand—maybe it's something simpler. Maybe someone needed the restroom."

"But they were here at the table. The restrooms are over there, pretty far away."

They fell silent again as they thought it over. Franza spoke first.

"What about her shoes? Why was there only one here?"

Felix shrugged.

"She must've lost it during the struggle—or whatever it was—and he didn't notice because he was panicking."

Another pause. They were trying to picture how she would have fallen, how her head could have hit the stone.

It started raining again. Franza closed her eyes and inhaled deeply. It smelled like a walk through freshly cut grass in summer.

She longed to take off her shoes and dig her toes deep into the wet grass, like she used to as a child. Back when the mornings were cool and big, when the creek was a raging river, and the days were filled watching the wide-open sky. She'd been crazy about those summers.

Felix nudged her. "Everything all right?"

She nodded. "What kind of struggle?" she asked.

"What was it about? Broken heart? Wounded pride? Jealousy?" Felix shrugged. "At least that's why a lot of people have snapped before. Those things could make someone go completely off the rails."

He ran his hand through his hair, trying to think. It was starting to turn gray and suited him well. "Yes," he said. "And that's when she fell and landed on this rock. Did you get a look at the wound on the back of her head? Borger thinks that's what happened. The impact would've knocked her out for a while."

Franza nodded.

"It was probably just bad luck, not what our man had planned. No one plans that in advance," Felix said. "But then she was just lying there, not stirring, not making a sound. And he panicked. Probably thought she was dead."

They fell silent. The air smelled of summer, of grass, of wide-open sky.

"What would a normal person do in this situation?"

"Get help. Or drive to the nearest place to get help, take the next exit, find a hospital."

"What did he do?"

"He seemed to have had the same idea. That's why he put her in the car and took off. At least for a hundred yards."

"Or he just wanted to get rid of her. He thought she was dead, making things a lot more complicated. Try to picture that. Suddenly you're stuck with a dead body."

They felt the weight of their words tugging at them. They could see it in her eyes. She hadn't been dead.

So someone had an unconscious girl in his car, unconscious most likely because of something he did to her, and drove away from the rest area and onto the autobahn. Then he suddenly slammed on his brakes so hard that the car shot straight from the shoulder onto the grass. Then he dragged the girl out into the open and took off, leaving her there to die. Why? Did he panic because the dead girl suddenly stirred, because the whole thing was getting more and more complicated?

"And then?"

"Then she must have come to. Woke up. Had no idea what had happened. Lying there on the grass, in the rain, in her sparkly dress, soaked to the bone, one shoe missing. It must have been cold."

They fell silent again, mulling it over.

"And then?" Franza asked again.

"And then," Felix said, "then she just started walking. Maybe she saw a light and was walking toward it. Wanted to stop a car, and took one step too many."

Maybe she was confused. Or scared. Maybe she thought she was being followed.

They didn't know. They only knew that the next moment Bohrmann was there with his BMW. As always, when Franza was confronted with confusing homicides—the kind that gripped her mind and swept over her, lodging in every fiber of her being— she found herself longing for childhood: the cool meadows, the little brook, the icy cold creeping up her little legs as she pattered through the water past the smooth pebbles.

She would cry on Port's shoulder. He would hold her. But none of that would help.

"If not him, then someone else," Felix said quietly. "She wouldn't have survived, not at that time of the night. Two hours earlier she might've had a chance. If only . . ."

Franza nodded. "She would have needed some luck . . ."

"But you know," Felix said slowly, "I don't think luck would've helped her in this case."

Franza looked puzzled. "What do you mean by that?"

He rubbed his chin, thinking. He'd forgotten to shave that morning, probably thanks to his wife, Angelika's, unexpected early morning news.

"Our witnesses, you know, this Dr. Franke and his wife, they observed something interesting. While the doctor was running to the accident scene, his wife stayed in the car to call the emergency number. That's when she noticed a car parked on the side of the autobahn, about fifty yards ahead on the shoulder. And then it suddenly took off, as if bitten by a snake, engine roaring. She said it seemed really strange to her, as if someone was fleeing the scene, so she told her husband and then told me. What do you think?"

Franza shook her head. She had seen and heard so many things in her job, but she never got used to it. So he had waited. He wanted to know what would happen, to see her run out onto the road and die.

"What kind of car was it? License number?"

Felix shook his head. "She didn't know. It was very dark. And it happened so fast."

Franza sighed. "Damn!"

Felix raised his index finger and smiled triumphantly. "Hang on," he said, "wait a minute. We walked up to the scene, Frau Franke and I. She used to be a runner and was pretty good at telling the distance. Now guess what I found."

He paused. Franza looked at him blankly. Cars whizzed past, heading north to Nuremberg, Potsdam, or Berlin.

"Cigarette butts," he said. "Several. Some hadn't even been lit, just snapped in half. Somebody must've been pretty nervous. Borger will compare them to the butts from around the table. If there's a match—and I bet we'll find one—we'll have our suspect's DNA."

Franza slowly tilted her head to one side. "All we have to do then is find him."

Felix nodded. "You don't think we will?"

"Yes, of course we will." Franza turned to leave. "Let's go. I'm wet enough as it is." *I can't grow any more anyway.*

As they walked back to the car, Franza's thoughts returned to the girl. "What if she'd gone the other way? If she'd run into the woods?"

Felix shook his head. "Then he would've thought of something else."

Silence. There was nothing left to say. It could have happened that way. It was always sad like that, every time. And the girl's eyes. Hazel eyes. Her matted hair. Her eternal silence.

10

"Angelika is pregnant again," Felix said.

"Wow!" Franza said.

"Is that all?" Felix asked.

Franza grinned. "Well," she said, "gotta expect that if you're doing it."

Felix gasped.

"No," she said, leaning forward and giving him a pat on the shoulder. "Just kidding. Good for you. Congratulations. Planned?"

Felix rocked back and forth in his chair, thinking. "I'm not sure, I think so. You know Angelika."

Yes, Franza knew Angelika Herz. A woman with both feet firmly on the ground, and now she was expecting their fourth child.

"And my eldest isn't eating properly," Felix said. "Marlene. Since she turned fourteen she hardly eats anything. Angelika says it's my fault. Because of this damn job."

Franza nodded and put her hand on his shoulder.

"Do you think so, too?" he asked.

"What?"

"That it's my fault."

She shook her head and squeezed him a little. "Oh, Felix," she said. "That's nonsense. At fourteen they just don't eat because they don't eat."

"Yeah, isn't that the truth!?"

Franza nodded and squeezed her colleague's shoulder a little tighter.

"She told me this morning, about the baby," he said. "Then I got the phone call about this girl, and I had to run. She wants to tell the kids and celebrate when I get home, but I'm not sure I feel like it."

He fell silent for a while. "I'm not even sure I want a fourth child."

Franza nodded. "Will it be difficult financially?"

He shook his head. "No, you know my in-laws with their business. It's doing pretty well, and Angelika is their only child. You could say we'll be wealthy people someday. Our house is big enough, too. Angelika planned for everything. But I . . ."

He got up and walked to the window. "I feel like a breeding stud," he said quietly, almost ashamed. "She didn't ask me."

Franza joined him, and they stood side by side looking out the window. They couldn't see beyond the house opposite them. It was late evening, and the air was mild after the rain, a little misty. The others had left and were probably sitting in some beer garden, scarfing down pizzas and salads. Somewhere out there the autobahn was buzzing.

They still had no idea who the girl was, but she wasn't in any of the photos in the missing persons file.

Her handbag with her ID was probably still in the suspect's car where she'd carelessly set it down after she got in and they roared off into the night. Perhaps she wasn't even carrying any ID, just a tiny purse with a lipstick inside. Who needs ID at a party? Who needs ID in the face of death?

No one else seemed to be looking for the girl. Not a single report had come in. They were still within the required waiting period, but people usually came forward sooner because they were too worried to wait.

Arthur and Robert, the two junior members of the investigating team, had done a computer search for any missing persons reports that fit the girl's description, a girl who failed to come home after a night out—but nothing. Absolutely nothing.

Strange, Franza thought. *There are no reports of this missing girl. Didn't she belong to anyone other than her murderer?*

Franza thought of the suspect as a *murderer,* though she wasn't sure that was the correct legal term in this case. No one had been murdered, not in the true sense of the word, not in a way that the act would necessarily be treated as murder.

Bodily injury resulting in death, failure to render assistance—that's probably how the case would be handled if it came to court, unless, of course, they could prove that the yet-unknown suspect was acting with intent, or they could make him admit it. But that was the least of their problems right now. First they had to find him.

"We'll get him," Felix said, sensing her unrest.

She smiled gratefully. "We will, right?"

They were a good team—tough, and with the necessary persistence that anger always gave them. First thing the next morning they would visit the hospital's morgue, where the coroner would carefully reconstruct every minute of the girl's death and explain everything clearly and calmly to Franza and Felix, as he always did. The forensic team would have some preliminary results, as well, which would allow Franza and Felix to meticulously track down all the leads until they reached a conclusion.

"Summer vacation starts soon," said Felix, shaking his head. "Time flies, it's incredible."

Franza nodded absentmindedly and thought how many times she'd heard him say that. She couldn't help being touched by his repeated astonishment at how quickly time flew by.

"Do you think it'll get even hotter?" Felix asked. "I know you don't particularly like the heat, but . . . it'd be nice for the kids."

Franza shrugged, wishing herself away, to Lapland or the Arctic Ocean. There were lights there, iridescent lights, far out on the ice. Will-o'-the-wisps with white halos, hissing and fizzing like sparklers, only brighter. And more dangerous. They were ghost lights, and if you walked toward them you would disappear. Franza wanted that sometimes on days like today. To disappear as if she had never existed. Just for a few moments. Into the ghost lights and away.

"Would you like some almond cookies?" she asked, pulling a Tupperware container out of her bag. "And my famous meringues? I have enough for both of us."

He laughed and shook his head. "Unbelievable! Have you been baking again?"

They gorged themselves, the cookies sweet in their mouths.

11

"I've been so many places," she said. "And it's always different from what you expect. It never is the way you imagine."

Ben didn't dare to move for fear her touch would dissolve into thin air, and then it would be as if it never happened.

"You're too scared," she said, smiling. "You're too scared to run off, to just jump with no safety net."

He didn't know what to say. Her hair fell down over his face, smelling of summer. He closed his eyes.

"But that's OK," she said so quietly he could hardly hear. "I was just kidding. It's OK that you're too scared. It's all right."

She let go of him and he instantly burst with longing for her, because he knew she wanted to leave—at once, this moment. He racked his brains wondering how he could keep her a little longer, but he couldn't think of anything.

She smiled, and he saw that a tiny, green piece of apple peel was caught between her teeth. "Can you let me out?" she asked.

"Already?" he asked and knew it wasn't enough.

"Yes," she said. "Already."

He nodded, pulled over to the side of the road, his thoughts with her, as they had been for days.

*She opened the door, her hand almost touching his. "You know,"
she said, "I've had enough of all this moving. I'm sick of it. You never
reach home."*

He had to clear his throat, and could only nod.

*"See ya later," she said, smiling. Her fragrance was that of a
breeze from the South Seas and the moon. "No," she said. "You
never get there."*

Then she was gone.

*Marie in the streetcar. No ticket. Tits like melons. Eyes like
apples. Never got home. That's Marie for you. Of course she didn't
have a ticket.*

12

On her way home, Franza took a detour past the theater where Port performed every night.

She'd never seen him onstage, didn't go to the theater. It wasn't her thing. She knew it hurt him although he wouldn't admit it. She knew he wanted her to come to the theater, to watch him and admire him. He was vain and arrogant when it came to his acting—like a faun. When they first met, it came as a shock to him to realize she didn't know who he was, hadn't seen him onstage, and didn't even recognize his name.

Franza smiled when she thought of it. He had tried hard to hide his dismay, but it had been obvious.

His apartment turned out to be an ideal retreat, apart from the lack of a coffeemaker, which she decided to do something about.

She stopped the car outside his place, leaned her head against the headrest, and closed her eyes. It would be hours before he got home, and he would be tired, possibly a little drunk. There was little point in waiting, but she sat there thinking it over anyway, and drifted off to sleep.

She jumped when her cell phone rang. It was her husband, Max. "Franza?" he asked. "What's up? Are you coming home? I'm cooking."

She couldn't help laughing. Ever since TV became full of those cooking shows and it was fashionable for men to cook at home, Max had begun cooking, too. He denied the connection vehemently, but Franza wasn't buying it.

"Yes," she said, and all of a sudden she was starving. "I'm on my way. Twenty minutes."

She hung up, sighed, and looked longingly up at the fifth-floor windows. Then she started her car and set off for home.

Port had guessed from the start that she was married. As with each of her affairs, she had announced on their first date: "I won't tell you anything. No name, nothing. Can we do that? Do you agree?"

Port had lifted the right corner of his mouth sardonically and raised the opposite eyebrow.

"Yes," he had said, "agreed. I know everything anyway, everything important. I know you're married, if that's what you're worried about. Anyone can tell from a hundred feet away."

"Really?" she had asked sulkily. "You can?"

"Yes. That's right."

That's when she had decided that whatever happened happened. But nothing dramatic happened. They just screwed. This, however, they did to perfection, and with passion, as if it were everything. And she thought, all right, so this is how it works, it just keeps going; there is nothing more to it than that.

She had been late for a meeting because of their first date, but she needed to breathe. After she had left him, she went down to the Danube, watching as it flowed by, smoothly but impatiently.

Franza thought, *so this is how it is now.* And she thought, *I don't know his name.* And she trembled. Just a little, but still.

Her cell phone rang again, startling her out of her daydream. "We're out of ketchup," Max said. "You forgot to get some. Could you pick some up?"

She looked at her watch. "Do you know how late it is?"

"Try the gas station," he said. "See you soon."

At home, the table on the terrace was set for a candlelight dinner. Franza was surprised. "Do we have something to celebrate?" she asked, as she put the ketchup on the table.

Max's face took on a serious expression. "Yes, you could say that. Since our beloved son doesn't seem to be remotely interested in dentistry, I sold the practice."

Bang. It hit home.

She stared at him, speechless, her jaw dropping. Then he burst out laughing. "God, you swallowed it! It was a joke! A joke! Do you seriously believe I'd ever sell my practice? What would I do all day? Cook?"

She turned around, picked up the barbeque tongs from the table, and threw them at him. He ducked, still laughing. "Are you trying to kill me? No, we don't have anything to celebrate, just a beautiful summer evening. And that we're both here. Don't you think that's nice? Franziska?"

He came closer and lifted his hand to touch her, but she drew back, just a little, but he noticed. She saw the suspicion in his eyes, and she tried to smile.

"Don't call me *Franziska*. You know I don't like it," she said, just for something to say as she sipped on her wine.

He fell silent and concentrated on cooking the food. He had not been his old, cheerful self for some time.

"Where's Ben?" she asked. "Have you seen him?" He shook his head.

She walked from the terrace into the garden, stroking her roses. Her son lived a life apart. Since she had accepted this fact everything was easier. She had stopped asking, "When will you be home?" If he was there, he was there; if he wasn't, he wasn't.

She had to consider carefully what she asked him about, which was difficult since it was her job to ask questions—precise, difficult questions, tough questions on the verge of indiscretion.

Once she had noticed that his lips were cracked. "How can you kiss with those?" she had teased. "Lips like sandpaper! Don't you kiss anyone?"

That had been too much. "Mother, please! That's none of your business!" he had said gruffly.

And then he took off, jumping into Max's second car and heading into town, leaving Franza just standing there. *Why is your love life none of my business,* she thought stubbornly, *when you were a result of mine?*

She knew that Ben was at loose ends. Since getting his high-school diploma last year on the second try—which they had all been delighted about—he had been drifting, trying this and that, but not settling on anything. It wasn't helping Franza's guilty conscience.

She had been living with it ever since Ben was born. She was never sure she had been there enough for him or given him everything he needed. She had gone back to work right after he was born, doing the balancing act between job and family, putting him in day care every chance she had. She hired au pairs from all over Europe, one of whom—a young woman from Sweden—felt responsible not only for Ben's welfare but also for Max's.

That had been the first breach of trust, a humiliation Franza couldn't get over for a long time. Max, of course, insisted it meant nothing to him, just a flirtation, a warm body in the cold of winter. Franza was never there, always preoccupied with her corpses, if not in person then in her mind.

During their crisis she had thought about divorce, starting over again, but somehow everything had stayed the same, except there were no more au pairs, and Ben suddenly insisted on being called *Ben,* not *Benny* or *Benjamin.* Ben. From that day on he was *grown-up.*

Franza often wondered if Ben had noticed anything at the outset or if he knew about the little Swedish girl who now would be about as old as Ben was at that time and who couldn't talk with her father in her own language because he couldn't even speak it.

That Franza even knew about the girl was due to a ridiculously mundane incident. She had picked up Max's suit jackets from the cleaner's one day, and the woman behind the counter smiled and handed her the clothing along with a photo of a little girl, a toddler, with Max's eyes beaming at the camera.

"This must be your little one," the woman had said, as she continued to smile. "Adorable. My granddaughter is the same age. It was in one of the pockets, and I thought you'd miss it, so I kept it for you."

Franza had stared alternately at the photo and the woman behind the counter, whose smile slowly turned into confusion. Finally Franza put the picture into her bag, said "Yes, thank you," and paid. Then she ran outside, jumped into the car, and drove around aimlessly for two hours.

That's how it had happened.

She hadn't confronted him. She had gone home, put the photo down in front of him, and retreated into her study with a cup of coffee.

It had taken an hour before he could bring himself to face her. They sat opposite each other, looking at each other, not saying a word. He brushed a strand of hair from her face, and she took hold of his hand and pressed it against her lips.

It was a farewell, they both knew it, and at first it had seemed easy. The pain came later, in the night, toward morning. She moved into her study and didn't sleep with him for a long time. Once a year he went to Sweden for a week, and she took a lover from time to time.

"Oh, I just remembered," Max called from the other side of the garden. "He called this morning."

Franza turned around. "Who?"

He looked up briefly from turning the chicken on the grill. "Ben, of course. Who else are we talking about?"

"And?" Franza asked, walking back to the patio.

"Oh, I don't know, we only talked for a minute. I was busy with a patient. He said he'd be away for a few days and we needn't worry. He would explain everything when he got back, and he'd have a nice surprise for us, something we'd be happy about. Something along those lines. It sounded promising, as if he'd made a decision."

Franza took a sip of the wine and looked at the meat, which had been on the grill for far too long now. It would be dry, which was just the way they liked it—one of the few preferences they had in common. "Really?"

"Yes, absolutely."

Max put the pieces of chicken on two plates and set them on the table. "Come, let's eat. Help yourself to salad."

He took the ketchup, squirted a big blob on his chicken, and looked pleased.

Franza cringed and felt her hunger disappear. "Hm!" she said.

Max took a long drink of his wine and leaned back, sighing contently. On the patio, they were sheltered from the gentle breeze wafting through the garden, while the wall behind their backs radiated the warmth it had stored up from the sun during the day.

"Wonderful, these summer evenings after the rain. Smells so good!"

Franza nodded.

"How does it taste?"

She nodded again. "It's excellent."

He squeezed her hand briefly. *I'll probably grow old like this,* she thought. And at eighty we'll still be fighting over who gets the ketchup from the gas station.

Crickets were chirping in the garden, and it was getting dark.

"What are you thinking about?" he asked.

"A girl who was murdered," she said.

He didn't respond. At some point he had lost interest in her cases. They were all the same to him. He didn't understand what for her was the basic rule of her job: death, when it happened, was always new and always different.

She knew he didn't understand and felt a sudden surge of tenderness toward him because he lacked this important knowledge. She looked at him and noticed that his hair was thinning and his shoulders slumping forward. On an impulse, she lifted her hand and touched his cheek gently. He looked at her in surprise. Then she thought of her lover and his director, and of the girl, and of the tears she hadn't yet shed, and she longed for Port's shoulder. She smiled.

"He called you, too, by the way, but your phone was turned off," Max said. "Why?"

She didn't react right away, but she saw the alert look in his eyes and took a forkful of salad before answering.

"Why what?"

"Turned off. Your cell phone."

"Oh, yes!" She dabbed her mouth and lifted her glass, aware that she was annoying him. "Was it? This morning? Oh, yes. The battery was dead. I had to charge it at the office."

She tried to sound casual and could sense she was failing and that he didn't believe her.

"How is Felix?" he asked.

13

"You still haven't cleaned this place up!" she said every time after she had to visit the morgue. She walked into his room and sat down on his bed, sighing. "You live in a pigsty. You come and go as you please. Your life is running through your fingers."

Now that, he thought, would be bad . . . if life were running through his fingers. Which it wasn't. Clearly not. Not anymore. Because Marie had noticed him. Finally. And she loved him. Life was good. Marie loved him. Finally. He scribbled on the paper.

Marie in the streetcar,
Marie, the lovely.
Marie, the tiny.
Marie in the streetcar.

. . .

What was that supposed to be? A poem? A love poem?

. . .

Only Marie has the key to my heart. Mouse rhymes with louse rhymes with Klaus.

. . .

What a bunch of shit! He laughed, shook his head, turned in his chair and made the room spin.

. . .

"It still isn't cleaned up," Franza would say. "You live in a pigsty; you come and go as you please. Your life is running through your fingers. Oh, Ben! Ben!"

She was away a lot. She'd had this job even while he was still very young.

"Chasing the bad guys!" his father always said with a touch of sarcasm.

And her voice was always the same when she said "Oh, Ben!" As if she were overcome with amazement.

He didn't make up the amazement part. Phrases like that never were one's own. Phrases like that were centuries old; they came ambling down through the centuries, listening with ears like a lynx, and at the first opportunity they latched onto the right coat like a tick. His coat was just the right fit. As if gripped by an overwhelming amazement.

He, Ben, collected phrases like this. He found it exciting, special. Like Marie. Except Marie was more special. She was the most special thing that had ever happened to him.

The bit of apple peel stuck between her teeth would already be on its final journey.

14

"Twins," Felix said looking miserable. "That will be tough."

Franza's eyes opened wide. "You're kidding!" she said.

"Nope," he said. "It's true. Even Angelika is shocked now."

They were drinking coffee from the vending machine. The coffeemaker had finally died, and no one had bought a new one. It was Wednesday morning, ten o'clock, and Franza had shown up for work on time, no detours to Port. She was haunted with thoughts of the girl, who wanted to be recognized, wanted her name back.

They'd gone through every missing person's report. Nothing. They would give her picture to the newspapers.

"She's due early November," Felix said. "Then we'll have five of them. Imagine that! Five! Unbelievable!"

He sniffled a little and shook his head. "She had an appointment with the gynecologist yesterday afternoon, and that's when she got the big news."

Franza pulled the container of cookies out of her bag. "Here you go," she said. "Our daily sugar ration. You can have it every day from now on if you want. Makes you happy."

He nodded and made a face. "I appreciate it," he said, "but I've got a toothache on top of everything else. Since yesterday. Since I ate those things you baked. I've hardly slept, popping pills all night. And then this news."

He groaned. "Do you think you could call your husband and ask if he can fit me in?"

She shook her head slowly. "I don't know," she said hesitantly, "if that's such a good idea. It could be more painful than necessary for you. Maybe you should look for a new dentist."

Felix looked at her with surprise. "Why is that? I always see Max."

Well, Franza thought, *if "always see" means every five years and only when it's urgent, then yes, "always see" is true.*

"You could almost say he is my family dentist," Felix mused aloud and examined his tooth with his tongue, the pill-popping finally having the desired effect.

"Explain," he said next. "Come on, out with it. You know who the expert is in questioning here. So, what have I done? Why can't I see Max anymore? Why can't Max touch my teeth anymore?"

Franza sighed and drummed on the desk with her fingernails. Ancient pictures of Max and Ben laughed out of an ancient picture frame. Even back then things hadn't been right. *All right,* she thought, *he won't let me get away with it anyway.* She swallowed and prepared herself. "I believe he thinks I'm cheating on him. And I believe he suspects you."

"Me!" Felix gave a surprised laugh. "Hallelujah! Now that's some news."

He took a cookie, nibbled carefully, pushed it into his left cheek immediately, and washed it down with coffee.

"And? Are you?"

"What?"

"Cheating on him."

Franza remained silent. Felix grinned and shook his head. "Franza, Franza!" he said. "You're something else."

They did it standing up, Franza and Port, they did it lying down or sitting, elaborately and precisely, as lovers do.

They did it like lovers.

They had been relying more and more on words lately. She didn't object. It felt dangerous.

"Don't you love your husband anymore?" Felix asked.

"I don't know," she said. "So much has happened over the years. I don't know."

Felix nodded like he knew what she was talking about. "We're past forty," he said. "Doesn't everything change then? Over and over? Doesn't everything have to change over and over again? And when you face death all the time . . ."

He took a sip of coffee, staring straight ahead. "Angelika," he said, "used to be scared a lot. At night. Lying awake. But not anymore. Now she has the children."

Franza nodded. "Yes," she said. "I know what you mean."

"The girl," Felix said. "I gave her picture to the newspapers."

"Good," Franza said. "Good."

15

The rippled surface of the Danube mirrored the trees on the bank. Occasionally, fish jumped in the clear waters along the edge. You could see rocks, sand, leaves, driftwood, and the shadows of the bushes at the bottom.

Yellow dots sparkled in the green meadow, sometimes purple, poppies glowing, elder flowering.

"Come!" Marie said. "Come here, my Ben!"

A jogger wearing a burgundy-red T-shirt dashed along the water's edge and was gone as fast as he'd come. Another came along, slower, exhausted. They heard his breathing, his steps. He gave them a nod, and they nodded back.

"I used to come here a lot," Marie said. "I loved it. The quiet, and that all you heard was the wind and the trees. And then the frogs croaking. Or the ducks. I can't tell the difference." She laughed.

"Frogs," Ben said, grinning. "They're frogs, you city slicker!"

"Is that so?" she laughed. "Country bumpkin!"

He put his hand on her arm.

"You're nice, Ben," she said in the middle of the kiss. "Will you come to Berlin with me? To wish me luck?"

"Yes," Ben said. "Of course. Of course I'll come."

He leaned back and looked into the sun. Everything was clearer when Marie was around. She was clarity personified to him, clearing his mind, his feelings, his life.

"I'm going to study biology," he said. "And when I'm finished, I won't get a job, because you can't get a job with just a biology degree. My father is going to sell his practice because I'm not taking over, and then he will generously give me a monthly allowance, which will see us through while you're becoming a famous actress. Someday you'll make it big, and then you'll bring home the money, and I'll be a stay-at-home dad and raise our children, and I'll bring them here regularly so that, when they're older, they'll know that frogs croak and ducks quack. By then, my father will have moved to Sweden. My mother will keep chasing murderers till the day she dies."

"Wow," she said, grinning. "What a plan!" She pulled him to his feet. "Come on!" she cried, "Let's jump into the water."

"What?" he squealed. "In the cold! Never!"

He put up a fight, they wrestled. "Let go!" he said. "Way too cold."

"So what?" she said, certain of victory. "We're wearing warm clothes!"

She pushed and pulled to get him in, and it was as cold as he'd expected. "You frog!" he shouted, and she laughed.

On the hill the yellow wheat rolled gently like an ocean, stretching far down toward the western bank.

After they hung their clothes on the bushes to dry, and the shadows had dissolved into the black mass that was the Danube, they made love. Her hair fell onto his face, and he buried his nose in it; he closed his eyes and felt her touch, which was like foam on the dark river waters.

16

The blood on the stones was the girl's, DNA analysis confirmed. Traces of her blood were also found on the shoes.

"Well!" the coroner said. "We have a young woman, early to mid twenties. Before the accident she would have been in relatively good health, maybe a bit malnourished, but that's nothing unusual for a female that age."

He stopped, raised an eyebrow, and grinned suggestively as he glanced at Franza's twenty pounds too many. She parried with an indifferent smile. "Look at yourself, Borger."

He cleared his throat, patted his belly, and continued to grin. "Whatever you say, Franza, my dear. Shall we go for a bite to eat later? You know I adore your hips."

He turned and grinned at Arthur, their young colleague, who remained discreetly in the background—not because he was discreet by nature, but because he was feeling sick to his stomach and trying not to let it show. "You know, I love her hips!"

Arthur had no choice but to return the grin, but didn't really know what to say. He hemmed and hawed and then finally mumbled, "They are nice hips." He cursed himself inwardly because he could feel how he was blushing.

Franza and Borger laughed, and Franza was surprised to see Borger looking Arthur up and down with interest. She was sure Arthur had noticed, too, and maybe that was why he'd turned red. Arthur was smart and easily drew the right conclusions. He had potential, and Franza and Felix were training him as their successor.

As their successor! That sounded as if they were almost ready to retire even though they still had a good twenty years to go.

But that's the way it went. They had to train good people, had to give them time to grow and to develop their instincts and personalities. That didn't happen overnight. It took time, and Arthur was someone they were willing to invest their time in because they had high hopes for him. He was hungry and tough when necessary, but he also possessed a certain sensitivity—a rare combination.

"Well," Borger said. "Shall we go eat?"

He turned to Arthur. "You're welcome to join us, of course." His voice quivered a little.

Franza shook her head and tapped her forehead. "How can you think of food right now?"

"Oh, come on," Borger said, "ever since you rejected me in favor of that gum plumber, I constantly think of food. Considering how cold it is in here"—he gestured around the room—"I have to keep up my strength."

She nodded and smiled, suddenly feeling a wave of calm and composure coming over her. She secretly called him tie-Borger, because she had never seen him without a tie. Every time she saw him she decided to get him an especially classy one for next time, but she always forgot. They'd known each other since their college years and had even lived in the same dormitory for a few months.

They liked each other, and their banter at the many wakes and burials they had attended made the deaths easier to bear.

"All right," he said, turning his attention back to the girl lying on the metal table in the hospital's pathology room. She seemed distant, more distant than on the autobahn, but Franza knew this phenomenon. Lying on metal tables beneath bright lights, they were pale and ashen, all color drained from them. Some took on a greenish hue. Often it was here the victims would regain their dignity—here, where it was returned to them. Even as every last secret was being stolen from them, their loss was atoned for by finding the clues to their death.

"So young!" Borger said, turning serious. "Sad."

Franza nodded, carefully taking a strand of the girl's hair between her fingers. Dark brown bordering on black. As she'd thought.

"And you still don't know who she is? No one reported her missing?" Borger asked, looking doubtfully at Franza.

Franza shook her head. "No, no one."

"Maybe she's not from around here. Maybe she's from God knows where and no one has missed her because everyone thinks she's gone on vacation. It happened on the autobahn, after all. Autobahns lead into the unknown."

For a moment Franza was astonished at Borger's poetry. She shook her head again. "I think that's unlikely. Would you go on vacation wearing a dress like that? Sitting in the car for hours? I can't see it. To me, it's precisely the dress that narrows our area of interest. But let's wait and see. Her photo's in the newspaper today."

"You're probably right," Borger said. "Shall we begin?"

Franza nodded.

"So," he began, "death occurred almost immediately, thankfully, you could say. The injuries were definitely fatal, and there was nothing anyone could have done. She didn't have the slightest chance."

He paused, remaining silent for several moments, and then continued. "The car must have hit her with full force. The pelvis and thighs have multiple fractures, everything is crushed. Moreover, some of the inner organs are pretty roughed up, too, meaning that several systems failed at the same time, complete shutdown, multiple trauma. Ruptured intestines, ruptured liver, ruptured aorta."

Borger fell silent and wiped his forehead with the back of his hand. A fan was humming on the ceiling. Arthur was trying to get used to the air, to the smell of disinfectant and chemicals, and to the indefinable something that seemed to be hovering in the room.

"What was the cause of death in the end?" Franza asked.

Borger looked at the girl pensively. "Loss of blood," he said. "A girl her age has about six pints of blood. It doesn't take long to lose that, only a few minutes."

He looked up and into Franza's face. *It affects her,* he thought, *yes, we're not getting any younger, this sad look about her mouth . . .*

"The blood on the stones in the rest area is hers, then. Can you elaborate?"

He nodded. "Yes, we were lucky. Insofar as after the collision she landed on the grass beside the road and her head and face received very little damage. There's only this one conspicuous wound on the back of her head, and that definitely wasn't due to the accident. The laceration caused the blood on the rocks that we saw."

He paused again, clearing his throat. "Additionally," he said, with unmistakable satisfaction in his voice, "I found tiny traces of moss in the wound. We can say with absolute certainty that it is the same moss that's on the rocks in the rest area."

He nodded a few times. Then he continued, "You see these marks?" He pointed to several dark bruises on the girl's throat.

Franza nodded slowly. "Strangulation marks."

"Exactly. She must have been strangled, and then fell or was pushed, and hit the back of her head on the rocks."

Franza frowned. "Did she try to fight off her attacker?"

"There's no one else's DNA under her fingernails, if that's what you mean," he said regretfully.

She sighed, and he studied her face again. *Yes,* he thought, *this is new, this look about her mouth, the tired eyes.* Her hair, however, was as blond as ever. Still shiny with the same reddish tinge, though maybe she just had a good hairdresser. *Well,* he thought with resignation, *it can't be helped, we're getting old.* And he realized with surprise how familiar the thought was to him, and how often he'd thought it before.

"What happened next?" Franza asked, noticing Borger's intent gaze. "She was lying there . . ."

He nodded. "Yes. And was most likely unconscious."

"Because of the impact."

"Because of a *commotio cerebri.*"

"Concussion."

He smiled mischievously. "Yes."

"And how long did this unconsciousness last? How long was she lying there?"

He thought it over for a moment. "Maybe half an hour. Probably less. However, she had a considerable amount of alcohol in her blood, which would've dulled her senses further."

"Meaning?"

"That I can't tell you precisely. It could've been less, but also more. But more likely less."

"Could he have thought she was dead?"

Borger stopped again to think, scratching his chin and moving his head from side to side. "Yes," he said finally. "Definitely. If you're not familiar with death, and if, on top of that, you're panicking, not in control of yourself, then yes, I believe that could happen."

"When she woke up, did she know what had happened?"

He shook his head. "Not necessarily."

"Temporary amnesia due to concussion?"

"That's right."

"And how far back would that reach?"

"Can't say for sure. But she certainly didn't know right away that she'd received a blow."

"That means she woke up and had no idea where she was or why she was there. She only knows it's dark and she's got a pounding headache. Something's wrong with her head. She touches her hair, feels something sticky and wet, and assumes logically that it's blood, because what else could it be. She panics, wants to escape from the dark, maybe someone's still lurking in the bushes, she hears the noise from the road, sees lights approaching, walks toward them and . . . bam!"

Borger nodded. "A realistic scenario."

Franza looked up from the dead girl on the dissection table and into Borger's face. "Was she raped?"

"No." Borger shook his head. "But she did have intercourse. No traces of sperm, however. A condom was used. But I've got something else of interest to you."

53

He lifted the dead girl's arms and turned them so Franza could see the other side. They were covered with scars both above and below the elbows.

"Wow!" Franza said quietly.

"You know what this is?" Borger asked.

She nodded. "Of course. Self-mutilation. She was cutting herself."

"You'll find plenty more on her inner thighs."

"How old are they?"

"Years. No fresh scars."

Franza picked up the sheet that was folded back on the girl's hips and pulled it up to her face, thinking *farewell, fly away home.* Then she carefully put down the sheet and nodded.

Borger understood and signaled to his assistant, who had waited discreetly in the background. The assistant unlatched the dissection table, wheeled it out of the room, and took the girl back to the cold storage.

"OK," Franza said. "That'll do for now. Can you let me know when your examination is finished?"

"Sure." Borger nodded.

"I'll go ahead," Arthur said from the back of the room, and they realized they'd forgotten about him. "I'll wait by the car."

"Everything all right?" Franza asked.

"Are you OK?" Borger asked. "Do you need a sip of water?"

Arthur held up both hands. "No, no, I'm all right. All I need is a little fresh air." And then he was gone.

"Well," Borger said, folding his arms on his chest and following Arthur with his eyes. "He's still young."

"Yes." She smiled, a little puzzled. "How about you?"

He pulled himself together, swaying a little. "Sure, sure. Well? What do you say? Would you like to come with me to get something to eat? There's this new Italian place."

She shook her head. "My life's complicated enough. You still haven't got a new girlfriend?"

He waved his hand dismissively. "They're only after my money. I'm a lonely man."

"My poor darling!" Franza shook her head with mock gravity. "That's really a shame!" She gave him a friendly nudge. "You probably stare at all of them the way you stared at me earlier. It's terrible! I always feel like one of your corpses. And today of all days, when I've hardly slept. I look ancient."

He started to grin and raised his right eyebrow. *Revenge is sweet,* he thought, preparing to deliver the final blow. "Not too old to catch the eye of one of our theater actors, people say."

She immediately turned red and stared at him, speechless. He enjoyed seeing how astonished she was.

"People are saying that?" she asked.

He lifted his hands reassuringly. "Don't worry; they're not shouting it from the rooftops. In fact, they don't say it at all. It's just that . . . my hearing is pretty good. Or rather, my eyesight."

He loved extravagant explanations that didn't explain anything but made everything even more confusing. She became impatient.

"And what is that supposed to mean?"

"That I saw you, that's all. At Marinello, on Gutenbergstrasse. About two weeks ago." He already regretted bringing it up. "His interest in you was obvious. And your interest in him . . ."

He broke off, suddenly embarrassed.

She nodded and realized that she was frightened and becoming even more so. Was that what she had wanted? To take the risk of being seen? By friends like Borger? Or even at some point by Max?

Did she want to hurt Max? To ridicule him by flaunting her lover in public?

Were her feelings for Max still strong enough that she needed revenge?

Should she end it? With Port? Or her marriage to Max?

Enough of this. Forget it!

Pushing the thoughts from her mind, she returned to Borger, who was staring at her blatantly again. "Hey!" she said. "You're doing it again."

He'd forgotten how to hide his interest in living faces and bodies a long time ago—forgotten after years of dealing with dead bodies that couldn't defend themselves anymore. But it just wasn't appropriate in civilized society.

She tugged on his sleeve. "You can't stare at people like that!" she said. "Won't you ever learn?"

Now it was his turn to blush. "I'm sorry," he said.

It was his job to examine people, but the living felt he was looking for faults. He really wasn't. Not always, in any case.

"Listen," he said, "I haven't told anyone about you and this actor. You can count on my discretion."

She nodded and turned to leave. It was cool in this greenish, metallic room. She shivered; it was uncomfortable.

"By the way, how do you know who he is?" she asked.

Borger laughed. "Well, my dear, isn't it obvious? I'm a person interested in cultural things, unlike you. Lots of people around here know him."

She looked at him thoughtfully.

"Have you even seen him onstage?" he asked disapprovingly.

"No," she snapped, "I haven't. I have to go. Arthur's waiting."

She was almost at the door when he stopped laughing and called her back. "Wait!" he said. "One more thing. Nothing too important, but still."

He picked up a pair of long tweezers, leaned over a dish and took something out. "We found it in her mouth. It must've come off her tooth when she fell."

A tiny silver piece of jewelry flashed in the fluorescent light.

"Tooth jewelry," he said.

She nodded. "I know," she said. "Young girls wear those things. Max offers it at his practice, too. Is that a moon?"

"Yes," he said, "a moon. It must've sparkled every time she laughed."

17

Marie wore the moon on her tooth and her eyes shined like apples. She danced through the arcades in the old part of town to the beat of the songs drumming in her ears through the headphones. When her phone rang the first time, she didn't hear it.

After she'd bought a doner kebab she sat down on a bench and turned her face toward the sun. She'd seen on the weather forecast it was supposed to rain that night, but for now it was a hot, bright midsummer day.

The kebab was a little hot, but it was tasty, and she felt the yogurt sauce running down her chin and starting to drip. She had to laugh, leaning forward as to not drip on her jeans, and finally wiped her mouth with the napkin.

When her cell phone rang the second time, she heard it. She swallowed quickly, dabbed her mouth again, and answered.

She listened for a while, slowly shaking her head. Her face took on an impatient expression. "No!" she said. "I don't think that's a good idea."

She hung up, wrapped up the rest of the kebab in the paper, threw it into the trash, and kept strolling in the sunshine.

Her phone rang a third time. She stopped, checked the screen, sighed, and then pushed the "Decline Call" button. Soon after, it rang again.

"Shit!" she muttered. "Why doesn't he get it? It's not that hard!"

She let it ring several times before she answered. "I don't want anything to do with you anymore!" she said angrily. "Is that so hard to understand?"

But the caller was persistent, and Marie gave in.

"All right!" she said. "But only because it's such a beautiful day and because the sun's shining. You know, I'm leaving in two days, for my entrance exam."

The caller appeared to object. Marie laughed. "But I can do it. How can you doubt that?!"

She hung up. The sky had darkened and it had started to drizzle. Lightly. Gently.

She ran through the raindrops, arms outstretched, thinking of her pearl dress, of the strings on the silver background. She jumped here and there through the drizzle, the water forming dark spots on her jeans and T-shirt. Silver pearls, she thought, pearls of rain on a silver background.

The rain became heavier, so heavy that the drops hit the asphalt and bounced back up. Frogs, she thought, little, transparent frogs, quacking, growing in the summer rain.

The train station came into sight. She rushed inside, bumping into an elderly man, sending his bag flying, scattering its contents onto the floor. Marie stopped. "Sorry!" she shouted and raised her hands apologetically. "I didn't see you."

"Well then don't run around like a headless chicken," the man grumbled.

"Yes," she said, helping to pick up his things. "I won't in the future, when I'm not in such a hurry."

The man shook his head. "You look like you're always in a hurry, young lady. Why don't you give yourself a little more time?" He gave her a kind smile as she packed his things back into his bag.

"Yes," she said and grinned. "I will. Take my time. Yes. When I've got time for it, maybe in another life."

He shook his head disapprovingly as she charged off to check the train schedule.

Later, at the mall, she put her head on a copy machine and copied herself. From the side. In profile. Several times.

As if she didn't want to forget herself. As if she wanted to be forever. Something forever. Something everlasting.

It was still raining outside, translucent, shimmering. She hopped around through the raindrops.

18

Strange guy, Arthur thought. *Borger. If I ever get like that, I'll shoot myself!*

He was glad to be outside. He crossed the road, leaned against the car, and held his face up to the sun. It seemed unavoidable that this job would get to him at some point, although he really couldn't complain about his superiors, Felix Herz and Franza Oberwieser. As far as he could tell, they had stayed relatively normal, so maybe it wasn't all that bad. They even had personal lives, in Felix's case even a rather productive one, three children, and from what he heard, more on the way. A few things were being whispered about her, too, but well, that's just police gossip.

He sighed and felt his thoughts turning to Karolina, knowing he shouldn't think about her, but as always, he couldn't help it.

He swallowed and sighed. Oh Karolina, insane body, beautiful long legs, flaming Andalusian eyes. Although she was born and raised in the ancient city of Straubing—a Straubinger—she worked at a video store, of all places, to pay for her education. It was the same video store where he chose to rent an innocent little porn video for an innocent little bachelor's evening. That didn't go very well. He had flirted with her right away. How could you not with a woman like that?

No. Hang on. Maybe he should stick to the truth. If he started lying to himself at this young age, he'd go downhill in a hurry.

She had flirted with *him*. Not the other way around.

If he was honest, and he'd just decided to be honest, he had to admit it. That it had been her picking him up, not the other way around. And if he was even more honest, he'd have to admit he'd never have had the guts to flirt with her. Not her. Not this incredible Andalusian woman from Straubing.

But oh well. Look where it got him. A broken heart and a policeman's split personality.

Five weeks of flying high, five weeks of not eating, not drinking, not sleeping. He hadn't known this was possible, and yet he lived—no, thrived! He had excelled in his work, or so he'd thought, but after four weeks they declared him non compos mentis—mentally incompetent—because he kept staring into thin air. The rings around his eyes had become too obvious.

Felix and Franza had pulled him aside.

"What's the matter, boy? Do you have trouble sleeping?" Felix asked.

"No!" he had wanted to say. "No!" he wanted to shout into Felix's concerned face. "I don't have time for sleep! I'm screwing! I'm screwing myself out of my twenty-six-year-old mind! I'm screwing the most insanely hot woman on the planet! I can't do anything else but screw at the moment! And I know it can't end well!"

Of course he hadn't said anything. Franza looked at him, and he could see in her eyes that she had an inkling, as if she knew what was happening to him, as if she understood. Since then he'd thought very highly of her. "Everything will work out," she had said. "You'll see."

He had smiled and nodded. She was a woman who knew what she was talking about. But that it would end this way? Bam! And over?

That had been three weeks ago. Three damned weeks.

He could see her in front of him as if it were yesterday.

Karolina. How she had moved to the Konstantin Wecker music. How she'd taken off her clothes and sent them flying through the room piece by piece. And how she'd taken off *his* clothes and sent them flying, as well. How she'd dripped warm honey on his chest and stomach, how she'd begun to lick it off, her tongue circling on his skin until he was vibrating, inside and out, like the strings of a piano, and how every little hair on his body had stood up, and not only them . . .

But then . . . his cell phone had rung.

And he had answered. Not until after the fourth ring, though. He had to. Felix would've killed him if he hadn't.

But Karolina had jumped off him as if she'd been bitten by a snake. While he was still on the phone, she'd grabbed his shoes and clothes—everything—and chucked them out the door. And she'd made it unmistakably clear that she'd never even dream of being the woman of a shitty policeman, always on call and no boundaries. Then she steered him gently but firmly out of her apartment, handing him a damp cloth through the crack in the door only after he'd exclaimed that he was sticky all over and felt like a licked postage stamp.

Then, to make matters worse, he couldn't find his boxer shorts, but Karolina wouldn't open the door again no matter how many times he rang the bell. While he tried to slip on his jeans and T-shirt as quickly as possible, he turned toward the closed door again. A little muted in consideration of the semipublic location but emphatically, he'd asked Karolina what on earth was wrong with her. Was she out of her mind? He was half naked, standing in a stairway in the center of town in the middle of the night. But she was unfazed.

Eventually he had driven to the police station, fuming, where his colleagues were waiting for him, impatient to get started with a late-night stakeout.

When Felix had started sniffing him and asked if he was trying out a new honey-scented aftershave lotion, Arthur had been ready to give up—to quit—but Franza told Felix to leave the boy alone. It was the prerogative of youth to try everything. She stressed *everything* with that ironic tone she pulled off so well.

Just in time, Felix had planted his hand firmly on Arthur's shoulder. "Don't even think about quitting, boy," he'd said. "You're in the right place here. Believe me, there are women who can handle our unsettled lifestyle. And they're not the worst."

Shit, Arthur thought, shaking his head. *There I was standing in front of the corpse of this girl, and what do I do? Wallow in self-pity! At least I'm still alive!*

He kicked a stone across the road, and it rolled until it finally hit the curb on the other side—and the foot of someone wearing sandals and just starting to cross the road.

"Shit!" Arthur blurted and looked up.

"I'll survive," Franza said indifferently, walking toward him and smiling. "Have you been in the dumps?"

He felt caught in the act. "No," he said. "What makes you say that?"

She gave him one of those looks he couldn't fathom, and which made him so uncomfortable he didn't know which way to look. She shrugged. "Female intuition."

Great, he thought, *that'll make things easier.* He opened the driver's door and was about to sit down when Franza said "Shoo! Take off!" and shook her head.

He froze and looked at her in bewilderment. "You'll have to take the bus," she said. "I have to get another witness statement."

He shrugged. "I can come, can't I?"

"No," she said unmoved, and got in the car. "You can't. Give my regards to Felix."

Then she sped off. He stood there, a minute, two, maybe more. "Women!" he said with a growl. Then he walked to the bus stop, kicking stones.

19

Port had the newspaper spread on the table. The dead girl was on the front page. She looked asleep. The headline above the photo read in bold letters: "Unidentified Woman Killed in Car Accident Under Mysterious Circumstances."

The article described the sequence of events, and also that the girl had already been injured, and probably was confused because of these injuries when she staggered onto the autobahn. The question was how she'd acquired those injuries, and they even mentioned *murder*. The article closed with the usual plea to the public for any information, particularly concerning the victim's identity, and provided a phone number.

As was customary in situations like this, several phone lines had been set up at the police station to cope with the expected onslaught of calls. There'd be a lot of irrelevant stuff to wade through, but at some point also significant things. They just had to separate them from all the dark and wild suspicions. It would be a hell of a job to check through everything, but Franza and Felix knew from experience that it was worth it, because sooner or later they'd come across an important piece of the puzzle.

"I know her," Port said, tapping his finger on the picture in the newspaper and looking at Franza with raised eyebrows. "Believe it or not, I know her."

He had called just as she was walking from the morgue toward the car. He wanted her to stop by his place, said he had something to tell her he didn't want to discuss over the phone. He'd spoken with a finality that didn't leave any room for contradiction, so she'd gotten rid of Arthur and headed over.

She hadn't expected this, however. She leaned forward and stared at him in astonishment. "What?"

He repeated. "I know this girl."

"And?" she asked excitedly. "What's her name? Who is she?"

He paused dramatically, just for a moment, brought the fingertips of his hands together, and turned up his mouth. "I don't know."

Franza felt the excitement draining from her body and being replaced by disappointment. *Shit,* she thought. "You're kidding!" she said.

He shrugged. "No, sorry. But I thought anything I could tell you might be important just the same."

They were sitting on his roof terrace drinking tea. He'd been at breakfast when she arrived, and in an hour he'd go to rehearsal and wouldn't be reachable until late at night.

He still didn't have a coffeemaker, and as Franza sipped her tea listlessly she decided once again to get one for his kitchen. Someone like him, she thought disdainfully for the thousandth time, someone like him and he drinks tea!

She sighed. "Yes," she said. "Sure. Fire away."

He knew the girl from theater, from the Pechmann to be precise, a bar not far from the theater where actors, singers, and dancers socialized along with those who wanted to be noticed by the artists. Was she one of them? Someone who hung around in the shadows of the artists to be a part of their lives? To make the boredom of their own lives easier to bear?

"No," Port said pensively. "No, she wasn't one of those. On the contrary. She was someone who demanded attention."

"How?"

"Hard to say. She had something . . . ambivalent about her, and she was pretty good-looking. Somehow . . . independent. Radiating freedom, as cheesy as it sounds. But lonely, always a little sad, and that's a pretty irresistible combination."

He laughed and bit into one of the croissants Franza had hurriedly picked up at a bakery.

Yes, she thought, *I can imagine. Irresistible combination. For you, too?*

She knitted her eyebrows and caught her thoughts drifting, imagining the girl and Port together. At disturbing places, doing disturbing things. Drinking tea, among other things.

"What did you say?"

He laughed and dipped the croissant into the jam. "Hey, what are you thinking about?" He leaned closer, and she could smell jungle, freshness, him.

"Here," he said, "tastes good," and stuffed the pastry in her mouth. The jam smeared all over her mouth, dripped, and she tasted apricot on croissant, followed by Port's tongue. She swallowed, choked, and had to cough. He laughed quietly and said, "You made a mess, Frau Inspector!" but didn't let go of her.

Shit, she thought. *What's going on here? What am I getting myself into?*

"So," Port said finally, leaning back. "The girl. I got talking to her once. She'd seen me onstage. She hated the production, but not me." He smiled mischievously.

Franza nodded. *Yes,* she thought, *I can imagine.* She put the teacup back on the table. *When I leave,* she thought, *I'll go buy a coffeemaker.*

Port was still grinning with the memory of his pampered vanity and stayed quiet for a while. Franza let him be. She knew from experience that it was better not to interrupt people when they paused, lost in memories. She knew he would continue soon. And so he did, after clearing his throat.

"During our conversation it became clear that she'd seen every single production of ours over the last year. She knew the parts and the plays well. She knew all about us actors, about the directors, the producers and—the most impressive part—she knew how to gauge us all very accurately. She had an eye for people and things."

I believe that, Franza thought, but at once sensed her own pettiness and felt bad, very bad. *She's dead, for God's sake. Put things back into perspective, you idiot!*

"Did she have money?" she asked. "I mean, so many shows. That can't be cheap."

"Standing room. Dirt cheap. But of course *you* wouldn't know that."

He grinned and reached for her. She nodded. "Yes," she said pointedly, "I know. You want to be admired." He grinned.

"What else do you know about her?" she asked, taking refuge in her job.

He thought for a while and shook his head slowly. "Nothing, I'm afraid."

"What did she do for work? A fellow actor, maybe? Since she knew so much about theater."

"No. I don't think so. Even though she was obsessed with theater, it wasn't her line of work. I would've known."

"Did she come alone?"

"I don't know. I wasn't watching her all the time, after all. She was just a regular, not a complete stranger. You know what it's like, someone walks past you every now and again and at some point you give each other a nod, sometimes you exchange a few words, but that's all."

"And you're sure you can't remember her name?"

He shook his head. "I didn't really have anything to do with her. I'm not even sure I ever knew her name. So many people give you their names, and they all expect you to remember. Do you know how exhausting that is?"

"Think anyway!"

He narrowed his eyes a little and sipped his tea, which had now become cold. "No, I'm sorry," he said and stood up. In the doorway to the kitchen he suddenly stopped, then turned around.

"Marie," he said, and seemed deep in thought. "Yes, Marie. Yes, I think that's it. Marie. That was her name. Marie. It had something light about it. I remember thinking that it suited her. Marie. Yes. Exactly."

He nodded and disappeared into the kitchen. Shortly after, he reappeared again.

"There was something sad about her," he said. "And something bright. And it wasn't yet clear which would outweigh the other. Nothing about her was decided yet."

Later, after Franza left, she thought of his words. Now, it was decided.

20

Franza entered the office she shared with Felix, sat down at her desk, and looked at Felix. He was on the phone. "Her name is Marie," she said, interrupting his conversation.

He looked up, stared at her briefly, barked into the receiver that he'd call back later, and hung up. "What?"

"Our dead girl," Franza said, realizing she was enjoying the surprise effect as much as Port had. "I've got her name. It's Marie."

"OK," Felix said, "now slowly, and from the beginning. Did Borger find the name scratched into her skin?"

Franza gave him a withering look and told him what she knew without giving any details about her source. When she was done, Felix leaned back in his chair, relieved.

"Well," he said, "that's something. We'll get there. Coffee?"

"Yes. I'd love some."

And then everything happened very fast. The phone on Felix's desk rang, and for some reason they knew immediately it was important. Felix turned on the speakerphone.

It was Robert. He'd been answering the phones. "Her name is Gleichenbach, Marie Gleichenbach. Her mother called. She recognized her in the paper."

21

They didn't talk much on the drive, which took them out of town to a small remote suburb. Franza thought of the caller, and tried to imagine what the woman must have felt like picking up the paper and looking into the dead face of her daughter. Unimaginable. She started to retch, but she swallowed it back, and the moment passed.

They pulled out into traffic on the A9 toward Berlin, and drove past the rest area where the girl—whose name at least they now knew—had received the injuries leading to her death. They took the next exit and followed a country road, past cornfields swaying in the wind like yellow waves in a yellow ocean. Finally they passed through a small wood and into the village where Marie's mother lived. It was afternoon when they arrived. The sun was hot, and it felt like there would be a thunderstorm.

Franza thought of the Danube and how nice it would be to lie in the shadows of the bushes, cooling off in the water from time to time.

"Yes," Felix said, as if he'd read her mind. "I'd rather be having a cool swim and a cold beer, too."

"Or coffee," Franza said. "Iced coffee." And she thought of the coffeemaker she bought when she'd left Port's. It was sitting on the backseat, still in its box.

The house came into view. It stood a little outside the village in the middle of a yard full of tall trees. They parked the car, rang the doorbell, and a woman appeared, standing silently in the doorway. Franza guessed she was about forty, with brown eyes and dark, shoulder-length hair, curling at the ends. An older version of Marie.

"Frau Gleichenbach?"

She nodded.

"Police," Franza said, trying to sound as gentle as possible. "I'm Detective Oberwieser, and this is my colleague Detective Herz. We're here because of your daughter, Marie."

The woman nodded, turned around, and walked straight through the house into the garden, to a group of chairs standing in the shadow of a chestnut tree. She sat down, gestured vaguely to two chairs, and Franza and Felix took a seat.

"Yes," she said, her voice trailing off into the trees. "I know why you're here."

Franza realized she hadn't offered her condolences and said all the things one says in a situation like this. "Frau Gleichenbach," she began, "I'm so sorry, but . . ."

She didn't get any further. The woman suddenly turned to the detectives and said, "I can't tell you anything. I don't know anything."

Her eyes flashed, and she drummed her fingers nervously on the arm of her chair. Felix ignored her irritation, cleared his throat, and asked the first question. "You didn't report Marie missing. Why not?"

"I wasn't missing her."

Franza and Felix were surprised but didn't let it show.

"You weren't? Didn't it seem strange to you when she didn't come home two nights ago, or the night after, or last night? Didn't you wonder why? Weren't you concerned? She wasn't found far from here. She must've been on her way to you. On her way home. Or wasn't she?"

The woman sat slumped in her chair, her face a white, vacant mask. When she tried to speak, her voice broke into a woeful moan. The detectives remained silent, waiting. She pulled herself together again.

"No," she said. "I don't think she was on her way here. I can't imagine it. She's been gone for a long time; she left us a long time ago. We never knew where she was. One day here, the next day somewhere else. She never stayed anywhere for long. Especially not here. Especially not with us."

She fell silent. After a while she continued. "I don't know what it was with her, why she was like that. Why it had to end this way."

Silence again. Suddenly she got up. "Come," she said. "Come with me."

They followed her back into the house and up a flight of stairs. She opened a door. A girl's room, very neat and tidy, with posters on the walls and books on the shelves. Curtains billowed in the open windows.

The woman walked up to them, wrapping herself into the fragrant fabric.

"I've just washed them," she whispered, "and hung them back up right away. This morning, after I saw the newspaper. And I opened the windows so it would be nice and fresh for her. Airy."

Her voice broke again. "Come!" she whispered finally and motioned to Franza to come closer. "Please come, smell them. Isn't it wonderful?"

Franza walked over and touched the woman's arm gently. "Yes," she said, "it is. You're right, Frau Gleichenbach. It really is wonderful." She took her hands and held them tightly. "Would you like to tell me your story, Frau Gleichenbach? Yours and Marie's? I'd like to hear it."

The woman nodded, and Franza sensed her relaxing a little. "Yes," she said. "Yes. That story. Mine and Marie's. I thought it was over."

22

Marie. Seven. Curly hair. Bundle of energy. Loved pasta and toast with Nutella. Went to school, liked her teacher, enjoyed learning, math, books. A bundle of energy.

At seven. But not since then—not for a long time.

23

"We didn't report him to the police," the woman said. "He was her grandfather, after all. He loved her, just differently."

She didn't know what he had done to Marie. Marie never said anything, and neither had the grandfather. But one day she came home from her grandparents and everything had changed. *She* had changed.

When Marie turned seven her mother began working in an office full-time and so she sent Marie to her grandparents' after school. She could do her homework there, and her grandparents fed her, played with her, and took her on short trips. It was a huge relief for everyone.

But then Marie began to change, became timid and fearful, cried at night, didn't laugh anymore.

At the time, her mother had thought maybe that's just how children got as they grew older. She thought maybe she was just imagining it. And then she blocked it out. Work was good; there was plenty to do. She didn't have much time, and in the evenings she was tired.

Then her sister-in-law came to visit, and when she heard that Marie was at her grandfather's every day . . .

She went to the grandparents' house, fuming. They could hear the shouting out on the street.

Then she took Marie aside and asked questions. Gently. Cautiously. But Marie didn't say anything.

Her husband said his sister was hysterical, always had been. They shouldn't pay any attention to her accusations.

The sister-in-law went back to England, where she lived, but before she left she had pulled Marie's mother aside and pleaded with her, "Don't let her go back there! Promise me you won't let her go back there!"

She had promised and didn't let Marie return, but it was too late. Nothing went back to the way it was before.

They didn't report the grandfather to the police. Her husband wouldn't have anything to do with the police, said it was his father after all, and an old man on top of that. He had one foot in the grave and who knew what his sister had made up—and now it was too late anyway. Not long after that the grandfather did actually die, and they were glad not to have started anything.

Marie was thirteen when her mother saw the cuts for the first time.

Marie had always worn long-sleeved shirts, but on that day it had been so hot she'd rolled up her sleeves.

Her mother had approached her from behind, and Marie didn't hear her. She stared at those arms, had never seen anything like it before, all those scars, so many scars.

When Marie had noticed her mother behind her, she lost it, became completely hysterical. That night she disappeared for the first time. Just like that.

They didn't find her for two weeks. At some point the woman had thought Marie was dead. She tried to feel it, but she didn't feel anything. She blamed herself for Marie's disappearance. Then they found her and brought her back.

"I can't remember," the woman said, "where she'd been." She tugged at the tablecloth with her long, thin fingers. "I wanted to forget."

24

They went back into the yard. Felix had brought water and glasses from the kitchen and was standing by the fence, watching the heaving of the yellow ocean, thinking of his children—of his skinny eldest—and how life could rain on your parade whenever it wanted to.

What have we done right, he thought, *and what have we done wrong, and will the right be enough?*

The women sat at the table, and the quiet voice of Marie's mother hung in the late afternoon air like a lament.

"Everything went haywire," Marie's mother said. "Sometimes she was here; sometimes she wasn't. When she was here, she went to school; when she wasn't, she didn't. We tried everything, but nothing worked. We despaired."

Social services got involved, the school psychologist—the wheels began to turn. Marie went through numerous institutions, state homes, private housing, charitable shelters, and every now and again was on the streets.

Then there was the last place. "I don't know," Marie's mother said, "what was different there, why she stayed. Maybe enough time had passed, maybe she was old enough, maybe it felt right to her."

But the fact was, she stayed. Appeared to have found something for herself. Went to therapy, went back to school, stopped the self-mutilation.

"She hardly ever came here," Marie's mother said. "So I went there regularly, to that house. Sometimes hiding just to catch a tiny glimpse of her. We opened a bank account for her, transferred money, the inheritance from her grandfather." She laughed bitterly.

Every now and then Marie would call on the phone. "I'm fine, Mom," she'd say. "Don't worry. I'm fine."

Occasionally—very rarely—she came to visit. The last visit had been the previous year, just before Christmas.

Marie's mother smiled at the memory, then got up and went back into the house. When she came back she put a piece of paper on the table. A letter-size copy: Marie in black and white, copied in profile.

So this, Franza thought, *was Marie without death in her face.* Eyes closed, probably to avoid the harsh light of the copier, closed mouth, the corners pulled up a little with the hint of a smile, hair that curled at the ends. On the back of the sheet were a few sentences, scribbled hastily in a moment of joy: *I'm going to the university, I'm in love, I'm racing the raindrops. I'll visit soon.*

"This came in the mail yesterday," Marie's mother said. "I was so happy. What happened?"

Felix came back to the table and sat down. "We don't know yet," he said. "But we'll find out. That's for sure. I promise you."

Franza looked up in surprise. Their eyes met. She raised her eyebrows. *Promise? He's that confident?* He nodded, just a tiny nod, barely visible.

Franza stood up. It had gotten late. Twenty after six. "We need a photo," she said. "Do you think you have one we could borrow?"

The woman nodded, got up, went into the house. While they waited they looked out at the fields. Franza longed for rain.

When they saw the photo, Franza thought of Port's pensive gaze when he described Marie. Everything he'd said was true, and she felt this tiny sting again, and just a little . . .

"Thank you very much, Frau Gleichenbach," she said. "We'll keep you informed."

She turned to leave. "Isn't your husband coming home?" Franza asked.

"No," Frau Gleichenbach said. "He hasn't been here for a long time."

Franza nodded. *What's life worth?*

"But shouldn't someone be with you? Can we leave you on your own?"

"Yes," Frau Gleichenbach said. "Yes. Of course you can. I know where she is now. And nothing can happen to her anymore."

25

Franza had bought chopped almonds and gingerbread spices. Now she was standing in her kitchen rolling dough. The first trays had already come out of the oven, and the room smelled of honey and cinnamon and ginger. Max stood in the door and bit into a chocolate-coated gingerbread star.

"Yummy," he said. "As always."

She nodded briefly. "Have you heard from Ben?"

"No," he said. "Why? Are you worried?"

She turned around, wiped her forehead with the back of her hand, and shrugged. *What's life worth?* "Probably not necessary, is it?"

He came closer, picked some dough from the bowl, and looked at her, shaking his head. "No," he said. "He's grown up and has gone away for a few days. That's what he said. I told you, remember? So what's the problem?"

She shrugged again, feeling helpless. What was it that Marie's mother had said? That now she at least knew where her daughter was?

"He's turned his phone off," she muttered. "I can't get hold of him."

"But he never leaves it on! He's probably lost it. Wouldn't be the first time."

She nodded, unconvinced. "Yes, probably."

He helped himself to a cup of cold coffee from that morning's breakfast. "No one could contact us when we hitchhiked through Europe," he said. "There were no cell phones. And we were younger than Ben. Our parents didn't worry themselves sick. I think your job's causing this."

Franza rolled the dough. It was just past midnight. "You're probably right," she said. Max took one last cookie and put it in his mouth.

"Of course I'm right," he said. "Also, you're working too much. And so am I. Therefore, I'm going to bed now. It's past midnight."

26

Ben's room badly needed airing. Franza tilted the window and picked up the dirty clothes strewn across the floor. Same as always.

Back in the kitchen, she slowly stacked dirty dishes in the dishwasher, cleaned the countertop, and put the cookies away. It was just before one in the morning.

She sat down at the window and stared out into the darkness. It was quiet in the house. She thought over what had happened that day, again and again. The nameless girl on Borger's table. Then Port's phone call and the name. Then her mother and her story. In that ancient garden full of trees.

Franza closed her eyes, fighting back her tiredness, and the pictures started to spin. The dress with the strings of pearls. Hazel eyes. Silence.

She thought of Port and that he'd known her, and that she didn't know how he'd known her, and also that she didn't know how far she should take her suspicions.

She realized Port had probably just gotten home, and she thought of the coffeemaker on the backseat of her car. *It should be christened.*

When she pulled out of their driveway, Max was standing at his bedroom window on the second floor, watching as she left. In the morning, he would find a note, hastily scribbled. *Have to go back to the office. Will sleep there. Don't worry.* He would shake his head and feel the quiet in the house, its size, its emptiness.

As she turned onto Port's street she felt a pressure in her stomach again: too many cookies, way too much coffee, and for the hundredth time she decided to see a doctor. "You'll end up on Borger's table," Felix had teased her, and Franza had forced a halfhearted grin.

She couldn't find a place to park in front of Port's building, so she drove around the block and parked on a side street. Probably better this way. Conceal and deceive was the motto. No one should discover her *second life*.

As she slowly walked back to his place, she thought about him, Port.

Maybe it was a stupid idea to show up in the middle of the night. He was probably asleep, dead tired from the work he did onstage night after night.

Maybe, though, he wasn't alone. Franza knew that was what disturbed her most: he could be with someone else, someone he gave more than just a word or a glance. Right now, at this very moment, for instance.

Maybe he had an actress with him. Or some admirer like Marie, who hated the production, but certainly not him.

Or maybe the director was with him, the director of the next play—Port wanted so badly to play the lead. Maybe he was earning the lead role right now and she'd be interrupting him.

What did Franza even know about him? And what rights did she have over him?

None. None at all, of course!

She shook her head in disgust, angry at herself for standing in front of his building—obviously in order to spy on him and obviously losing control over herself and her feelings. *Shit*, she thought. *Shit!* And she longed for his hands on her skin, in her hair.

What was hiding behind the actor's relaxed, handsome face? Behind his mocking eyes? When he raised his eyebrows she never knew what he was thinking. But his hands on her skin were honest, and his body was the most real thing she could imagine at the moment.

It sucks, she thought. *It sucks to be a woman, and not just an inspector-robot, a boss-robot, always in perfect working order.*

She stepped up to the entrance of Port's apartment house and leaned against the huge door. Shivering with cold, she rubbed her arms and shook her head again.

What kind of dark places was she carrying around inside her, what doubts? And he, Port? Did *he* have any dark places?

What time, for example, had he gotten home the previous night? Before midnight? After midnight? Early morning? And if so, what had he been doing all night long? Hadn't he looked weary when Franza stopped by, shadows in his eyes? And was it maybe *his* heart that was black as the night? She simply didn't see it because she didn't want to see it.

She inhaled sharply, longing for a cigarette or a glass of schnapps, something to hold on to. She felt the nippy air. It was still quite cold at night, and she pressed herself against the door, shivering.

What was she even thinking? Where was her professionalism? Her unfailing sense of judgment she used to be so sure of?

Maybe she was simply . . . jealous?

Could it really be the fact that Port had talked about Marie, the *way* he'd talked about her, that threw her off balance and brought her here now, to his apartment in the middle of town in the middle of the night? Was it just to make sure he was still Port, the Port she thought she knew inside and out?

She thought with a little melancholy about how it all began. She hadn't wanted to tell him her name, and he couldn't settle for that. "You have to see," he'd said, "that it can't work like this. I want to think of you by name. I can't think of you as *the nameless one*."

"Why are you thinking of me at all?" she asked. He rolled his eyes.

In the end, he simply had made up a name for her, called her Lea.

At first they met out of town at a motel along the autobahn. Every time she had thought it was the last time. But there was always a next time.

Once he had brought a picnic basket full of things to eat. She didn't like it.

"Why are you bringing food?" she asked. "Are we hungry? No, we're not. So why are you bringing food?"

He just laughed at her annoyance. "Do you only eat when you're hungry? Lea?"

He had stressed the name strangely, almost a little maliciously. She felt irritated and somewhat embarrassed, but she helped herself anyway.

Later, he ate strawberries off her belly with obvious enjoyment. She had nuzzled his neck lightly but she didn't allow herself any real tenderness.

"You won't do that again," she had said later. "I don't want you to do that."

"What?" he asked, surprised. "What?"

"The food!" she said. "I don't want this food. I just want to fuck, that's all—just fuck, screw, bang. Whatever you want to call it."

He was pissed off and shook his head. "You talk like a man," he said, "and you have no idea."

"Is that so?" she sneered. "Why not talk like a man? We're long past women following their men around like dogs."

"If you say so," he said grimly. "You can have your fuckscrewbanging."

She could taste the mold on the wall and his anger behind her. It had clung to her until she saw blue shadows. She liked it.

She hadn't allowed herself tenderness in a long time. The occasional gentle touch maybe, but nothing more.

She didn't allow him any, either. He couldn't become her shadow. She didn't want to walk through life fulfilled only by him, surrounded by the glow of his love like a Madonna.

She just wanted sex, a little action now and then—sex was healthy and saved you from going to the gym. If he started acting like a prima donna, complaining about her callousness, demanding romance, and turning up with strawberries to put on her belly, then he wouldn't last long.

That's what she had thought. For a while. At first. But soon she couldn't get enough of him.

When she took a shower he liked to watch her. He sat on the toilet, head in his hands. He couldn't understand why she didn't like that, said that washing oneself was as cold and clear as any porn, so she should like it.

So they did it. Twice a week, sometimes more. As often as they could. They fucked. It wasn't anyone's business, only theirs. When she closed her eyes his back tasted of Portugal. The Atlantic roared in her ears.

She'd been there once, more than twenty years ago. It had been the pits, *nil, nada, niente.* She always had sand in her teeth, the wind blew nonstop as she gazed toward Africa, and there weren't any decent guys around to make the situation better.

She didn't have any photos from that trip, hardly remembered how steep the cliffs had been, but Port's back gave her a vague feeling of having seen it.

Every time, she had sworn there wouldn't be a next time. But there always was, and eventually she told him her name. He just grinned and nodded, and she had a strong feeling he'd already known anyway.

He had given her the address of his apartment on the fifth floor of a house not far from the theater. The building was occupied mostly by artists like him: actors, singers, painters, writers—people from all around the world.

Once Franza had gone to visit him late at night, after a long day on an exhausting stakeout, and she'd sat with Port's neighbors in his apartment, talking and laughing in different languages—Russian, English, Spanish, whatever. Although Port had welcomed and introduced her very naturally, Franza couldn't shake the feeling of being a stranger in a foreign, unreal place. It saddened her because it showed her plainly what she'd suspected all along: namely that they were living in different worlds.

There were lights in his windows on the fifth floor; she could easily see that from the street. So he wasn't asleep yet, but was he alone?

Franza pulled her phone out of her bag and dialed his number. He picked up right away.

"I bought a coffeemaker," she said. "Can I set it up in your kitchen?"

It was quiet on the other end, and she sensed his surprise and a little hesitation.

"Now?" he asked eventually.

"Now." she said.

Silence again. *I'm dying,* she thought. *Please God, let me die.*

"Yes," he said. "Come on."

He was leaning in the open doorway when she came up the stairs. She didn't look at him but just walked straight by him into the kitchen and heard him closing the door and following her. She unwrapped the coffeemaker, plugged it in, rinsed it out once, twice, and then she put in a filter and ground coffee. It smelled delicious even before the hot water ran through. She wished he would come closer, but she realized he was waiting, waiting expectantly.

"What's going on?" he asked. "At this hour of the night?"

She took a deep breath, closed her eyes, and felt him even before he touched her. Then he was there, behind her, wrapping his arms around her, and she snuggled up to him, to his warmth, turning around to face him. She felt miraculously comforted.

"What's going on?" he asked. "What's the matter?" She finally broke down, crying into his hair, into the hollow of his shoulder, which smelled of the night and of losing oneself, of letting go— and when she finally let go, her bad conscience returned, and her fear.

The coffee was brewed, and she forced herself to let go of Port's shoulder. She could feel clearly, like never before, that one day she would be broken, her bones would fall to pieces one at a time, her skin a pathetic pile of tenderness, at some beach she loved, lost and gone. Finally they made love, no longer fucked. They hadn't fucked for a long time now.

For the first time it was crystal clear to her. It didn't surprise her, but it hurt, because it pushed Max out once and for all and she didn't know where he'd land—in a soft meadow or on a concrete floor.

Later on the dark terrace, they shared a croissant, which had gone stale during the day, and more coffee, this time with vodka, so that even Port liked it.

Marie had been in the dark, too, but on her own and close to death. *Moribund* as Borger would call it: "*Moribund, as we Latin students say.*"

Her thoughts wandered, and she decided to ask Borger if he'd ever thought he might be gay, because somehow he never got along with women.

"Do you think Borger is gay?" she asked Port, and remembered in that instant that Port didn't even know Borger, and she felt a new lightness inside her and had to laugh.

"Who?" Port asked. "Borger? Who's that supposed to be?"

Franza kept laughing, the vodka having gone to her head, and she tried to imagine Borger with a man, tie-Borger in bed with a man—no, that didn't work, that really didn't work, the thought was absolutely absurd, but somehow it wasn't.

She waved her hand dismissively. "Oh, no one, it's not important."

"Then why are you grinning like that?" Port asked. "Come on, tell me!"

"Your director," she asked. "Does he wear ties?"

He raised his eyebrows. "*My* director!" he said. "*My* director isn't *my* director. And yes, sometimes he does. Why?"

"Just asking," she said. "Just asking," and continued to grin. Maybe they could hook him up with tie-Borger.

After all, he was crazy about art and artists, as she now knew. Kill two birds with one stone. Borger's miserable single life would be over, and the director wouldn't be making eyes at Port anymore.

"So, little witch," Port said, throwing a cushion at her, "why this diabolical grin? What do you have up your sleeve?"

She threw the cushion back at him. "Your director," she teased, "will forget all about you once he's seen my tie-Borger."

After they tussled a little and landed in a corner of the couch, he said, "But I need *my* director, as you call him. I have to convince him. I want to be Hamlet!"

He paused theatrically and struck a dramatic pose. "To get this role," he said, "to get this role, Frau Inspector, any serious actor would commit *murder. Murder!* Do you understand?"

She moved her head from side to side, undecided.

"Well, maybe I wouldn't go that far," he said. "I'd only fuck!" He giggled, the vodka having had its effect on him as well. "But I'd do a good job of it. Why not? I've made love to men before, onstage. What's the difference?"

She pretended she hadn't heard it, the subtle irony in his voice, the little digs.

"Are you worried?"

She ignored it. "Hamlet?" she asked. "Is that the guy in love with his mother?"

He sighed. "No, dearest. That's Oedipus. Did you play hooky a lot in school?"

"Who cares," she said. "It's always the same story. They die and murder as much as they can, and in the end they're all dead. And you're fighting for a role like that?"

She sat up and looked at him. It had gotten so late she was dizzy thinking about it.

"Well," he said. "That's your field, too, really. Death."

"Yes," she answered. "True. Can you get the vodka?"

When he returned he was swaying a little. "You're jealous!" he said, and she could hear how surprised he was. "You're actually jealous!"

Now she was surprised herself, because she knew he was right, and she stared at him, for seconds—an eternity—and she felt her heart beating like a drum. *To die,* she thought, *now. Forever, and not have to deal with anything anymore.*

She grabbed her jacket and her bag, and headed for the door, but he jumped up and blocked her path, holding her tight. "No!" he said. "No. Stay, please."

She stayed.

Back on the terrace, they drank some more and ate the freshly baked cookies she'd brought with her. It had become quiet down on the street, and patches of light were appearing in the darkness. It was muggy; there'd be a thunderstorm, a downpour that would hit the street and bounce back up as little drops of water and evaporate back into the air, back into the wind, a never-ending cycle.

Marie, Franza thought, *was racing the raindrops.* That's how she'd been, a bundle of energy, and she'd probably won the race.

"Once, we almost got very close," Port said so quietly she could barely hear. She knew immediately he was talking about Marie, and she felt the sting, firm and sharp, a tugging pain.

This must be telepathy, she thought, *what a fragile idyll.* Deep down she wanted to laugh, but then fear took hold of her.

"You did?" she asked, trying to sound interested, like a detective should.

"Yes," he said. "For a brief moment. A really brief moment. But then one of us hesitated, and it was over."

He fell silent, thinking about it as she waited expectantly, looking into his eyes, unfathomable darkness. *Fragile idyll,* she thought again, *shit, shit!* She had the metallic taste of that fragility on her tongue.

"I don't even know who," he said finally. "Her? Me? Both of us? Do you know what I mean? A fraction of a second and you choose life or death, but you don't know, not in that moment."

She had pulled herself back together and tried to laugh. "Aren't you being a little dramatic? Choosing life or death! Shouldn't that be onstage?"

"No," Port said. "Stage! Life! What's the difference? Why are you making fun of me?"

She stroked his face gently, tracing the lines of his cheeks, his nose, his mouth. *I love you,* she thought. "*We* didn't miss the moment, this magical fraction of this magical second."

For a long time now they'd been making love, not just fucking anymore.

27

A nap, she thought. *A nap would be really nice right now.*

Unlike Port, who was still asleep, she had to get up and go to work. She knew she'd be irritable today, and she knew later she'd have to apologize to Felix and Arthur and Robert and everyone else for her foul mood. She decided to knock off punctually that night and get ten hours of sleep.

Things were already hectic in the office. Her colleagues were examining, organizing, and checking up on the calls coming in.

"So!" Franza said in a cheerful tone meant only to cheer herself. "What's up?"

"Lots," Felix said. "Really quite a lot. Did you have trouble sleeping? You look awful."

He shook his head and watched her as she rummaged around in her handbag looking for aspirin.

"Thanks," she said. "That's very sweet of you, Felix. Just think how you'll be feeling in a few months."

He grinned rather unhappily, and she was satisfied.

"So," he said, "let's take a good look at Marie's life. I figure her last home is most important. The manager called us, a social worker. She recognized Marie from the photo. Robert spoke to her, and apparently she's pretty shaken. He's made an appointment for us to see her this afternoon."

He leafed through the little notebook he always had on him, and then raised his head and stared at Franza. "Ah, yes," he said, "before I forget. We have a DNA match. The cigarette butts from the shoulder of the autobahn are from the same person as some of the ones at the rest area. Just as we suspected. It's nobody we have in our files, however, so he didn't do us that favor."

Felix shrugged regretfully and continued leafing through the notebook.

"What else? Oh, yes, a teacher called us, also because of the picture. She was going to school again and was in his class. I think we should talk to him, too. We're meeting him at the school around noon, during his lunch hour."

He flipped another page and nodded contently. "That's it for now. No one saw her on the autobahn, unfortunately. Or at least no one's contacted us about it. But you never know . . ."

He shrugged, leaving the sentence uncompleted, and took a sip of Coke.

"Yuck!" Franza said. "How can you drink that stuff!?"

Felix looked at the glass in his hand with surprise. "Why? Because of a few teaspoons of sugar? Your cookies have at least that much."

He turned around and walked back toward his desk. Before he sat down he turned to Franza again. "Oh, yes, the mother, Frau Gleichenbach, called again. She's coming to identify the body today and would like you to be there. I said yes. Is that OK with you?"

Franza nodded. "When?"

"She'll be here in about an hour. I thought you could drive to the hospital together."

"No problem."

She looked around the room. "We still don't have a coffeemaker?"

Felix kept typing on his computer without looking up. "No. I thought you'd bought one. I saw the box in the back of your car yesterday." He looked up. "Or was I mistaken?"

Franza felt herself turning red. *Shit,* she thought. "No," she said, "I mean yes. No."

He was listening attentively now, leaning back in his chair, rocking and grinning. "So which is it?"

She didn't answer, but sat down at her desk opposite Felix and turned on her computer.

"Ah!" he said, lifting his left eyebrow a bit and smiling. "I see. It was for . . ."—he thought for a moment—"for your . . . what do you call it? Lover? Do I know him?"

"How's Angelika?" she asked.

"Don't change the subject!" he said.

She was silent for a while as he looked her up and down. Finally she took a deep breath and decided to talk. Felix was her best friend, so who could she confide in if not him? She told him Port's name, convinced Felix wouldn't know it. But he whistled softly through his teeth. "Wow!" he said. "You've got good taste. Our theater's rising star! But since when do you have a thing for artists? You've never even been inside a theater."

She was speechless. Who else here knew Port? "How on earth do *you* know him?"

He laughed. "Why on earth are you surprised?"

She shrugged. "I don't know," she said. "*I* didn't know who he was." She had to grin. "That was a shock to him."

"I believe that," Felix said, grinning as well. "But by now he's probably used to the fact that you're a lowbrow. You must have other qualities, then? Qualities I don't know about?"

She narrowed her eyes and smiled mysteriously. "It looks that way."

"So the coffeemaker is at his place now?"

Franza nodded.

"Tea drinker?" He shuddered. "Unbelievable!"

Franza nodded. "Isn't it?"

"And Max?"

Franza sighed.

At that moment there was a knock on the half-open door, and a man entered: about fifty years old, well-groomed, a tennis-court tan, wearing a suit and tie and carrying the beginnings of a paunch.

"Am I in the right place?" he asked. "I'm looking for the detectives in the case of this girl, Marie Gleichenbach."

Felix leaned back in his chair again. The ball had started rolling. "Yes, you're in the right place. I'm Detective Herz, and this is my colleague Detective Oberwieser. And you are?"

"Lauberts," the visitor said, holding out his hand to Felix. "Dr. Lauberts."

He smiled a little apologetically and looked around. Franza got a chair for him and offered him a glass of water. "One never drinks enough, right? Especially in this heat."

"Yes," he said, grateful for this easy opening. "Thank you."

"So," Felix replied, putting an end to the formalities whose sole purpose was to put visitors at ease. "How can we help you?" he asked, and crossed his arms.

"The newspaper said it was murder," Lauberts blurted out. "And then it said it was an accident—so which was it?"

"Well," Felix said, "we don't know all the details yet, but there's a lot of evidence to suggest the girl's death was premeditated."

"Murder, then."

"If that's what you want to call it." Felix looked at the man with interest. He was clearly struggling with himself.

"And you're investigating?"

Felix nodded. "Yes, of course."

Lauberts took a sip of his water and sighed. "Well, in that case," he said, "in that case, I don't have a choice."

The detectives waited. Lauberts pressed his lips together and stared at his hands.

"Well, then," he began finally. "The thing is, I work for social services looking after adolescents who've gone astray, if you want to call it that. It's an administrative job, but I'm responsible for sending them to state homes and residential groups, which is how I met Marie Gleichenbach several times."

He paused and looked expectantly at the detectives.

Franza noticed that little drops of sweat had formed on his tanned forehead. "Yes?" she asked softly.

He emptied his glass in one gulp. "Well, the thing is," he said. "I want to be completely open with you. Each home we supervise has to keep a record of visitors. We can't have just anyone come and go as they please."

Franza and Felix nodded sympathetically.

"I mean," Dr. Lauberts continued eagerly, "it's our highest priority to keep our teenagers away from drugs and violence. We try to supervise their contacts as much as we can. This is difficult because they're not locked up, so they have to report to their resident supervisors, if you know what I mean."

Franza and Felix nodded that they understood.

Dr. Lauberts was on a roll. "After all, they're supposed to be rehabilitated. Of course, they can go wherever they want in their spare time, don't get me wrong. We can't control every minute of their lives anyway. But at least the comings and goings at the homes need to be recorded, who visits whom for how long, and *especially* when the visits take place behind closed doors, if you know what I mean. Certain acquaintances from our charges' pasts are not welcome at all, of course. I mean, I don't want you to think we're that suspicious, or that nosy, or that coldhearted, but our colleagues in the field have seen so much . . ."

He lost his train of thought and blushed under his tan. *How many hours has he spent sweating on the tennis court for this?* Franza thought.

"Now what are you actually trying to tell us, Dr. Lauberts?" Felix asked in a friendly tone.

He's good at that, Franza thought approvingly, *he really is good at that. When he wants something he can be friendliness personified—so nice, so kind, and soon the good doctor will have poured his heart out, and he'll have done so gladly.*

She shot Felix a smile and was certain that Dr. Lauberts was feeling quite at ease with them now.

"Well," Lauberts said, sighing deeply. "I'm here so you don't draw the wrong conclusions."

"Wrong conclusions from what?"

"Well."

He squirmed nervously on his seat. *Now we're getting down to business,* Franza thought. *Spit it out, we don't have forever.*

Felix smiled gently and glanced at Franza while Lauberts pulled himself together.

"You'll find my name."

Felix leaned forward. Franza held her breath as the suspense grew.

"Your name. Where?"

Now it was Lauberts's turn to become impatient. "Well, in Marie's visitors' record, of course."

"I see," Felix said, curbing his excitement. "Meaning?"

"As I said before, I don't want you to get the wrong idea!"

"And what would be the right idea?"

Felix's eyes had become narrow slits. He leaned back in his chair, rested his chin in his hand, and stared at Lauberts.

Lauberts stood up and began pacing back and forth.

"Please sit back down," Felix said calmly. "Why are you so nervous?"

Lauberts took a seat again. "I'm not nervous," he said. "It's just that I'm a little embarrassed. I mean, I don't usually visit my clients in their homes, or, more precisely, in their rooms."

"Yes," Felix said slowly. "That's a little embarrassing, indeed, especially since Marie is dead now. But that you showed up here on your own to explain the situation does you credit. So what was the reason for your, let's call it *visit*, to Marie?"

Lauberts sighed. "Well, it's not that easy to explain."

He looked pleadingly from one detective to the other, but the expressions on their faces remained impassive. He sighed again and took a deep breath. "She came to see me in my office one day to complain about the conditions in the home. She thought that Frau Hauer, the resident supervisor—have you met her yet . . . ?"

He looked questioningly from Franza to Felix, but they both shook their heads. "Yes, well, she thought that Frau Hauer was neglecting her duties, and that the place was getting out of hand. She said she didn't want to put up with it. I was surprised, especially because I know and value Frau Hauer as one of my most committed and able colleagues. So I agreed to come around in person to have a look at the situation, which I did. Unfortunately, Frau Hauer wasn't there, hardly anyone was there actually, only Marie and a new employee, an intern I hadn't met yet. She didn't know me, and insisted on putting my name in Marie's visitors' record even though I'd already shown her my ID from the social welfare office! But I didn't want to cause trouble, so I let her put my name down. You know what it's like, one has to lead by example—and when you haven't got anything to hide, like me . . ."

He laughed nervously and got up. "Well, that's it, really, that's what I wanted to tell you. That you shouldn't be surprised to find my name in the book."

He looked at his watch. "Yes, well, er, I should be getting back to work."

They felt his relief that it was over, but they weren't finished with him yet.

"You went into Marie's room?"

Felix's voice sounded calm and harmless. Lauberts nodded, a little confused, not yet realizing that he was digging his own grave. "Yes, I was supposed to inspect it."

"What about the door? Did it stay open?"

He started stuttering. "No, yes, I don't know."

"Which is it?"

He squirmed.

"Sit back down, please," Felix said. "So, the door?"

Lauberts stood still, but his face twitched.

"What was the name of the woman who wrote down your name?" Felix pulled out his notepad and a pencil.

"I already told you, I didn't know her!" A glimmer of hope showed on Lauberts's face.

"No problem," Felix said calmly and put down his paper and pencil. "Frau Hauer will be able to tell us. How long ago was your . . . *visit*?"

Lauberts closed his eyes for a moment, his breathing shallow. "Two weeks," he said flatly. "Maybe three."

"Well, not so long ago. Your conscientious colleague will certainly remember you and your . . . *visit*, don't you think, Dr. Lauberts?"

Felix got up, stepped behind the empty chair on the other side of his desk, and gestured for Lauberts to take a seat again.

"All right," Lauberts said and sank down on his chair, a picture of misery.

"The door," Felix said.

"Yes, the door. Marie might've shut it. I'm really not sure. Why is that so important, anyway?"

"There we are," Felix smiled. "The memory is truly a fascinating thing! We just have to jog it a little every now and again, don't we? Now tell us once more so we won't forget it again: the door was shut. Was it maybe even locked? What were you actually doing in that room?"

"Nothing. What do you think I was doing? Nothing, I just had a look around."

"For how long?"

"What do you mean—*how long*?"

"Well, just how long were you in there? That's a simple question, isn't it?"

Felix leaned over his desk and looked straight into Lauberts's face. The man blinked and then just gave up, his face ashen. "What's the point, you'll find out anyway. It's in the record, after all. About half an hour."

He was sweating heavily now.

"Half an hour!" Felix whistled softly through his teeth. "Isn't that a bit long just to inspect a room? Franza, what do you think? Isn't that a little long?"

Franza nodded. Satisfied with himself, Felix continued, "Why don't you tell us the truth about your visit to Marie's room, Dr. Lauberts?"

Lauberts paused for one more moment—one last attempt at resistance—and then he collapsed. "She tried to seduce me, the little bitch!"

"And?" Felix said sweetly. "Did the little bitch succeed?"

Lauberts protested. "Listen, I'm married!"

"That doesn't stop most people," Felix said calmly. "But I'm sure you know that as well as I do."

Felix fell silent. They were all silent. Then they entered the next round.

"Well, did she succeed?"

Lauberts paused to think. He pulled a handkerchief from his pocket and wiped his forehead. The detectives waited.

"You don't have to tell my wife, do you?"

"No, not necessarily."

Lauberts cleared his throat, squeezing the handkerchief in his hand.

"It only happened a few times."

"What?"

Lauberts looked up, surprised. "Well, I guess you can figure that out."

Felix shot up from his chair and slammed his hand on the table. There was no trace of kindness left in his voice. "Damn right I can! But I want to hear it from you!"

"Well then!" Lauberts sputtered. "I fucked her! For half an hour! Fucked, get it? Because she wanted it! Because it gave her a kick to do it in her room while that stupid twat waddled around out there in the hall!"

He stopped abruptly, shocked, and got hold of himself again. Then he continued quietly.

"I didn't even want to; I thought it was too dangerous. But that's how she liked it, always in strange places. In my office, in her room, at the lake with people all around, in the women's room at the mall. She always got me into the most impossible situations, the little bitch."

He shook his head, trembling all over, and took a deep breath.

"But you obviously enjoyed these . . . impossible situations. Otherwise you wouldn't have gone along with it."

Lauberts crumbled, nodding slowly. "You have no idea what it's like," he said, "when a girl like that comes on to you." He closed his eyes for a moment. "So young. Like a fountain of youth, like a . . ."

He broke off. He was melting like ice cream in the sun, but neither Franza nor Felix felt sorry for him.

"She was put in your care. Do you understand that?"

He nodded.

"And you took advantage of her."

He nodded.

"Did you kill her?"

Lauberts started as if bitten by a snake. "No!" he shouted. "For God's sake, no! Why would I do that?"

"Well, maybe she threatened to tell your wife. Maybe she was blackmailing you. Maybe she was tired of being your—what did you call it?—fountain of youth."

Lauberts squirmed on his chair. "I didn't kill her! I could never do such a thing! What do you think I am?!"

Felix didn't answer the question but posed a new one. "Where were you Monday, from ten at night until Tuesday, around five in the morning?"

"At home, asleep."

"Can anyone confirm this?"

Lauberts shook his head slowly. "No, I was alone in our house. My wife's on vacation in Italy, and our children are in boarding school."

Felix nodded. "You can go now."

Lauberts stood up, surprised and relieved. "So you believe me?"

Felix narrowed his eyes and didn't answer right away. "We'll see."

Lauberts nodded, took a couple of steps toward the door, and then turned around.

"I paid her, by the way," he said. "Just so you know. Good money."

Wow, Franza thought, raising her eyebrows. She looked at Felix and saw he was surprised, too.

Lauberts kept talking, his voice bitter. They stared at him, wondering what would come next. "And in case you're thinking it was just me . . . ! No, no. I don't know how many *friends* she had, and I don't know their names either, but there were a few. I'm sure you'll find that out. And one more thing: she was worth it, she was a born whore. She could drive a man to ecstasy, if you know what I mean. Really, it's a pity she's dead."

Lauberts edged his way to the door.

"Dr. Lauberts!" Felix said. Lauberts turned around again.

"That'll cost you at least your job."

Lauberts nodded, opening the door.

"Lauberts!"

He waited.

"Tomorrow, ten o'clock, here. Someone will take down your statement. We'll be expecting you."

Lauberts nodded again and left.

"Asshole!" Felix said softly.

Franza pulled out the container of cookies, fetched two coffee cups, and poured some Coke from Felix's bottle for them both.

"Ten years," she said. "Maybe even fifteen."

"What?"

"That's how much he aged in the last few minutes."

Felix grinned. "That's exactly what I needed now," he said, "your sense of humor."

He stretched out his arms heavenward and exclaimed in mock desperation: "Please God, look after my Franza and her cookies!"

Then he reached deep into the jar, pulled out a chocolate-coated gingerbread cookie, and put it in his mouth, chewing blissfully. "Do you realize this is perverse?" he asked.

"What?"

"Christmas cookies in summer. Chocolate-coated stars when it's about ninety-eight degrees."

"You think?"

He nodded with his mouth full, grinning. "I think."

"But you like them."

"True."

"You see? Then it isn't perverse. Being a cop, you should know how the human mind works."

He laughed and leaned forward, patting her arm. "We need to get a drink sometime soon, just you and me."

She nodded, got up, and walked to the window. Even though the windows were closed and the blinds were down, the thermometer read seventy-five degrees, and that was inside. She sighed and turned her thoughts back to their visitor. "Interesting, what he told us. Do you think it's true?"

Felix knew immediately what she was thinking. "What reason would Lauberts have to lie to us? None."

"Exactly."

"And her mother's statement, and the letter saying she was in love—how does that all fit together?"

"It doesn't. These are two different things."

"At least now we know what we need to look for."

"Something like a list of clients."

He nodded. "Exactly, a list of clients. Well, I wonder if we'll have any surprises?"

He picked up the photo and studied it thoughtfully. "I can imagine she was hard to resist."

"You can?"

"Oh, yes, looking at the picture—I'm just a man, too."

He raised his shoulders apologetically and looked at her with big, innocent eyes. She thought of Port and what he'd said, and in some far corner of her brain she wondered whether he was on the list, too . . .

"So what have we got," Felix said. "On the one hand prostitution and on the other, true love. Thank God she got to experience that, too."

"Poor girl. Don't you think, Felix? All those crazy locations— that's just crying out: 'I want to be discovered! Why won't you find me?!' What a legacy to inherit from your grandfather."

Franza paused for a moment. "We should try to spare her mother all this."

Felix nodded.

"We also need to check her finances as soon as possible to get a better picture of her . . . *job*."

Felix nodded again, slowly, thinking. "And her boyfriend, I mean her real boyfriend, I wonder who he is? We really need to find him."

"Which won't be easy."

"Why not? She was living with other young people after all, and they would gossip and share secrets, wouldn't they?"

"I don't think she'd have paraded him around much. The way I see our girl at this stage, she would have kept him secret, like the rest of her life basically. And if he hasn't reached out to us by now, I don't think he'll contact us at all."

"Which doesn't really reflect well on him. I mean, you kind of notice when you can't get hold of your girlfriend anymore. And if you have nothing to hide, at some point you start looking, you go to the police for help—but that *point* has come and gone, don't you think?"

"Yes," she said slowly, realizing she was thinking of Ben. Somewhere deep down in her heart she was thinking of Ben, and she was surprised.

"Maybe he discovered her double life and snapped. Don't you think that's a possibility?"

She remained silent, gazing into thin air, and he tapped her on the shoulder. "What's the matter?"

She came back. "Yes," she said. "Of course that's a possibility. What about Lauberts?"

"What?"

"His alibi without an alibi."

He shrugged. "I don't know. I haven't made up my mind about him yet. But at least he came in voluntarily."

Franza shrugged. "Could've been calculated, a strategy."

"Yes," he said. "One of us should be present tomorrow when they take his statement and give him another good grilling."

He took a sip of the Coke and made a face. "This is disgusting, warm as hell. We really need a coffeemaker."

Franza nodded. Then the phone rang on her desk. She picked it up and listened. "I've got to go," she said. "Marie's mother's a little early. She's waiting downstairs."

28

Her husband was with her.

If Franza had harbored the least suspicion he had something to do with his daughter's death, it was gone now. He was the opposite of what Franza had expected: a small, almost frail man wearing a dark suit and a black-and-white striped tie. Sorrow showed in his face.

Marie's mother stood silently beside him. She just nodded at Franza, and they didn't talk on the way to the hospital, either.

Perhaps, Franza thought, *this had been their mistake, not talking enough, keeping silent.*

Borger was expecting them. As always, he wore a tie under his white coat. Today it seemed appropriate.

Marie was back on the table, silent. As if she'd given all her answers, as if she were awaiting her release, when they would finally leave her in peace.

But not just yet, Franza thought. *I can't leave you in peace just yet. There are too many secrets you haven't told me yet. Talk to me, Marie, where is your boyfriend? Talk to me!*

But Marie stayed silent.

Franza turned away and looked at Marie's mother. She was calm, but her husband had to sit down, pressing his hand to his mouth.

"When can we take her home?" she asked, all the blood had drained from her face.

She'll pass out in a minute, Franza thought, *very soon, I bet.*

She looked at Borger, knowing he was thinking the same thing. He cleared his throat. "I've finished my examination," he said. "Now we'll have to wait for the results. Two or three days. I'll make all the arrangements to send her home."

"No!" the woman said, shaking her head. "Please don't. That's for us to arrange. It's the only thing we can still do. We'll take her."

For a brief moment she put her hand on Marie's hair, on her cheek, and then turned away abruptly, probably frightened by the unexpected strangeness and cold, and walked away. All her remaining strength left her and her knees buckled.

Borger caught her. He'd stayed close to her because he'd seen it happen so many times before. He did the only thing he could do; he caught her.

A moaning sound came from her lips, a drawn-out, quiet whimper, and Franza thought of the cornfields of Marie's childhood—the yellow oceans they'd seen along the road to Marie's home.

"We never asked her to forgive us," Marie's mother whispered. "We should have. But we were too busy feeling sorry for ourselves."

"Come on," her husband said. "Let's go. It's over. Let it be over now. Finally."

29

After dropping off Marie's parents at the train station, Franza stopped by an appliance store and headed back to the office, feeling good about herself. As she opened the door, the smell of freshly brewed coffee greeted her. Surprised, she looked at the small table by the window where the old coffeemaker used to be—and indeed, there was a new one bubbling away, exuding a divine smell.

"But," Franza stammered, "how did this get here?"

"I thought you'd probably need a decent cup of coffee when you got back," Felix said. "So I sent Arthur to get one. How was it?"

"Awful!" Franza said. "As always." And she put the bag with the coffeemaker she'd just bought on Felix's desk. He looked into the bag, leaned back, and laughed quietly.

"Sometimes," she said, "you know, sometimes I feel like it gets harder the older I get."

"Yes," he said, "I know."

30

It was a typical school. Old and a little run-down, with long, narrow buildings, crumbling plaster, and lots of posters and pictures on the walls. The corridors were so long you'd get lost in them if you didn't know your way and small classrooms were filled with students of all ages hollering and fooling around. Ancient couches in corners were supposed to provide recreational areas.

"I'm glad I've got that over and done with," Felix said. They walked up the stairs to the second floor, where according to the diagram, the teachers' room was supposed to be.

"Why over and done with?" Franza asked seriously. "Your children aren't even all born yet." She spread her arms and spun around as she walked down the hall. "If anyone's not over and done with this yet, it's you! Be prepared."

Felix forced a grin. "Well," he said, "if you put it like that, you're right. But maybe not all kids are as difficult as your Ben."

She looked at him sympathetically. "I hope so, for your sake." They both thought briefly of Marlene, Felix's eldest daughter, who was about to turn herself into a stick by refusing to eat.

When they arrived at the door to the teachers' room, they knocked and entered, but no one was there.

Felix grabbed hold of a teenager scooting past them. "Herr Reuter, where can we find him?"

The boy turned around and pointed back to where they'd just come from. "Down at the end of the hall. The Reuters have lunch duty on Thursday. Anything else?"

Felix nodded. "That's all, thanks." Then he stopped short. "*The Reuters*? Are there more than one?"

"Well, he and his wife. Is that a problem?"

Felix held up his hands and shook his head. "No problem, heaven forbid!"

The boy gave a quick wave and started to leave. "Hang on!" Felix said. "What are they like, the Reuters?"

"I only know him, really," the boy said with a shrug. "He's all right. English and chemistry. Not exactly my thing, but that's not his fault. Is that all?"

"Yes," Felix said, "that's it. Thanks, don't let us keep you."

The boy tapped his cap with his fingers and was gone. "Well," Felix said, "that's promising, at least."

Franza smiled indulgently.

The noise became louder as they walked closer to the big lunchroom.

The room was packed with students between ten and eighteen years old, and contained several pool and foosball tables. It was loud but bearable. Two adults, a woman and a man, were in the middle of all the activity. The woman was surrounded by a group of laughing girls who looked to be about fourteen years old, while the man was at one of the foosball tables, playing a game with three older teenagers. Franza and Felix made their way across the room to him.

"Herr Reuter?" Felix asked. The teacher looked up, nodded, and stopped playing. A student who'd been watching took his place.

"Yes," he said. "Johannes Reuter. We spoke on the phone, didn't we?"

Felix nodded. "Can we find a quieter place to talk?"

"Of course," Reuter said. "I'll just let my wife know."

When he came back, he wore a friendly smile. *Not bad,* Franza thought. *A nice-looking man, just my type.* She looked at Felix and knew he could read her mind.

"Your wife?" Felix asked as they were walking back to the teachers' room.

"Yes," the teacher replied. "She works here, too. Does that surprise you?"

"A bit."

"It's more common than you think. You meet in college, and the rest is history."

"And your children, are they here, too? Family business?"

Reuter laughed. "Not yet, they're too young—but who knows."

When they reached the teachers' room, Reuter held the door open for them, and they entered and took a seat. Reuter leaned over the table to serve coffee, coming close to Franza. He smelled freshly showered, but with a slight odor of coffee and cigarettes. She liked the combination immediately. She thought, *Wow, it's past noon, eighty-five degrees, and while the rest of us are sweaty and gross, he's . . .* and she closed her eyes for a fraction of a second. When she opened them again Felix was staring at her, grinning and winking. She made a face at him.

"Well," Reuter asked, as he sat down with them, oblivious to their exchange, "How can I help you?"

"Just tell us," Franza said. "Just tell us about Marie, anything you can think of. Anything might be important."

He became serious, leaned back in his chair, and folded his arms. "Well, what can I say? It's a tragic story."

He paused a moment, and a shadow passed over his face. It made him look more attractive, and Franza wondered how often he'd cheated on his wife. Wasn't it a law, after all, that good-looking men around forty cheated on their wives? Was that why she was working at the same school, to keep an eye on him?

"Marie started here two years ago," Reuter continued. "She had to take some tests and was placed in my class. She just completed her final exams—with average results, but who really cares."

"In her case probably no one anymore."

"Oh, yes, of course. I'm sorry. I haven't gotten used to it yet." He lifted his hands regretfully.

"What do you know about her past?"

He thought it over for a moment. "About her past? Not much, to be honest. I know she lived in a state home and for whatever reason she'd led a very unsettled life for years. We get all this paperwork from the welfare office, you know, but it doesn't really give you any insight into the life of a person."

He paused, brought his fingertips together, and continued slowly. "I was worried at first how she'd adjust to my class. I wasn't overly pleased to have her. I mean, you have to understand, it's not easy to join a class of sixteen-year-olds when you're twenty or twenty-one. But they managed really well, though she never fully became a part of the class, as far as I could tell from a teacher's perspective. She was always very late in the morning—too late— and in the afternoon she took off right away. She just never fit in with her classmates, not just age-wise, but mentally—just the whole way she was. But she was a nice girl, no doubt about it."

"How was your relationship with her?"

He laughed, a little surprised. "Me? Just a normal teacher-student relationship. I treated her just like everybody else. Sometimes it worked, sometimes it didn't—you know what it's like. But I liked her. She had special eyes."

He stirred his coffee, appearing genuinely shaken. *Perhaps,* Franza thought, *Ben just had the wrong teachers.* She sighed and felt sorry for herself for a minute. Thankfully that part of their lives was over.

"Don't you want to know what happened?"

The question came quick and sharp as a razor. For a brief moment the teacher seemed thrown. Franza looked at Felix with amusement. He always managed to throw the people he interviewed, every single time—and then he was secretly proud, but only she knew it.

"Yes!" Reuter said. "Of course! But I read the paper, and there's been a lot of talk at school, so I think . . ."

The door swung open and the woman from the lunchroom came in.

"Oh, Karen," Reuter said, and seemed a little relieved. "These are the police."

The woman walked over, nodded, and gave each of them a weak handshake. Though she seemed smart and was pretty, there was something obsequious about her. Franza was now certain that he cheated on her.

"We'd like to talk to her classmates," Felix said. "Is that possible?"

Reuter smiled regretfully. "Difficult, very difficult. All the students who finished their finals have gone God-knows-where.

Why should they hang around? We already had the official graduation party, too."

Franza and Felix looked at each other, the realization striking them both at the same time. The dress. That's why she wore the special dress.

"On Monday night?"

Reuter nodded. "Yes. The evening she . . ." He faltered, his eyes flickering briefly, and then he got hold of himself again. "How did you know?"

The detectives waved dismissively, not wanting to waste any more time with explanations.

"What was she wearing? Can you remember?"

Reuter shook his head. "What she was wearing? What a question. No, I really don't know."

Then his wife spoke up. "But I do. She stood out because she looked so . . . special. Maybe even a little overdressed for the occasion. But it looked good on her. She wore a dress, silver fabric, sequins, strings of pearls hanging down. A bit of a twenties style, if you know what I mean, those beautiful flapper dresses."

She was looking at Franza, and although Franza had no idea what she was talking about, she nodded. "There was something really special about the way she looked," Karen Reuter continued. "I think a lot of people noticed."

She broke off and looked at her husband thoughtfully. She smiled at Felix and helped herself to coffee.

"Well," Reuter said apologetically and smiled. "I didn't notice anything. Or I forgot. When you have so many students . . ."

He glanced at his watch. "Are there any more questions? I'll have to get back soon."

"No," Franza said and thought it was intriguing the way the sun bounced off Reuter's dark hair. She was sure he had a melancholy tendency and could lose himself in dark sonatas by Russian composers. "No more questions, thank you. But we do need a list of names and contact details for her classmates."

"I don't think that'll help much," Reuter said. "As I said, as far as I know she never had much to do with her classmates."

They got up. "Still," Franza said, "we'd like the list. You never know. Please?"

She smiled and Reuter shrugged. "Of course, if you say so."

They walked back down the long hallway, past classrooms with crammed desks and bookshelves. Suddenly Felix stopped and turned around.

"Oh, Herr Reuter," he said, looking closely at Reuter, "before I forget, apparently there were a number of men paying Marie for special services. Do you know anything about that?"

If Reuter did know anything, he hid it well. "Special services?" he asked, frowning. "What do you mean?"

Cute! Franza thought, *sweet innocence.*

Teachers! Felix thought, *no idea about the real world.*

Then it dawned on Reuter, his eyes growing wide. He shook his head in shock.

"What?" he said. "Prostitution? You mean prostitution? Good Lord, what are you talking about?"

"Now we've stolen his innocence," Franza said sarcastically as they descended the stairs.

Felix laughed. "She had him clearly convinced—and you said she wasn't an actress?"

She gave him a nudge, and he laughed, bounding down the stairs two at a time. When they opened the massive old door at the bottom, the sun beat down on them. Felix shielded his eyes from the sun and asked, "Maybe check with your actor friend?"

At that moment her cell phone rang.

31

It was Arthur.

"Bohrmann!" he said in a shrill voice. "Bohrmann's losing it!"

Franza didn't understand at first. "Bohrmann?" she asked. "Who's Bohrmann?"

"The guy from the autobahn!" Arthur shouted. "Jens Bohrmann, the guy involved in the accident! He's gone completely nuts. Barricaded himself in his house and holding his wife at gunpoint. He says he'll kill her if you don't come right away! He wants to talk to you, right now! And only with you!"

Something went off in Franza's head, and she understood. "Shit!"

"Hurry up!" Arthur shouted. "Don't waste any time, damn it, just come!"

They started running. Franza shouted the address to Felix and hung up on Arthur. They jumped into the car and sped away from the school, lights flashing and siren wailing, followed by the frightened eyes of the students and teachers who'd run to the windows.

It was a quiet street in the suburbs with small, pretty houses and flowering gardens—a peaceful idyll. Then they saw the crowd of people gathered around the police cars, which were parked chaotically in the middle of the road. Uniformed policemen had cordoned off the area and were pushing back curious onlookers. Members of the SWAT team, who were heavily armed and wearing bulletproof bodysuits and helmets, were strategically positioned around the house at doors and windows, waiting for instructions. The team leader, Major Andresy, was standing with Arthur on the front lawn of the house. Arthur breathed a sigh of relief at the sight of Franza and Felix.

"He called and wanted to talk to you, but we told him you weren't there. Then he started going on about how he'd blow up himself and his wife, and you were going to have to live with that," Arthur said, as Franza was helped into a bulletproof vest. Robert, who was a bit like Arthur's shadow, handed her a cell phone. A line was already open to the house, but Franza barely recognized the hoarse voice at the other end when the man from the autobahn said hello.

"Herr Bohrmann!" she said. "This is Franza Oberwieser, Homicide Division. You wanted to talk to me. I'm here now, and I'm coming in—take it easy."

The curtain on the window next to the front door moved slightly.

"I can see you," Bohrmann replied, opening the door a crack. "Put your hands up."

With her hands up as he'd instructed, she squeezed slowly through the crack, feeling so calm she almost made herself shudder. She thought of Ben, of Port, and of Max—in that order.

But when she saw the gun pointing at her, she felt her heart start to pound, and realized she was scared. She thought of Port and his warmth and could feel her strength coming back again.

As she stepped closer, Bohrmann moved back toward the living room, which was in semidarkness, the curtains drawn. The woman tied to the chair looked strangely out of place in the stylish upscale surroundings. Her face was contorted with fear, and she stared at Franza with wide, pleading eyes. "Help us! Please, help us!"

Franza nodded. "We will. Now calm down. Are you hurt?"

His wife shook her head vigorously, but it was obvious he'd hit her.

"Is anybody else here? Children?"

She shook her head again. "No, they're in kindergarten. He took them to kindergarten before."

"Very good," Franza said. "That's very good. You don't have to be afraid anymore, Frau Bohrmann. We'll end this now."

She turned around and looked again at the gun pointing at her. "Isn't that right, Herr Bohrmann? We'll end this now."

He laughed, and when she looked into his eyes she wasn't sure how they'd end it. His world had turned topsy-turvy, and the look in his eyes told her he didn't know which end was up anymore, that he wasn't sure he'd ever get back on even keel again.

"Sit down," he said harshly.

She took a chair and moved it alongside his wife. She was about to sit down when he stopped her.

"Stay away from her," he said. "Sit over on the couch."

"Herr Bohrmann," she answered as she did what he told her. "Jens. Don't you want to tell me what happened?"

"The gun! Put it on the floor!"

She stretched out her arms. "I don't have a gun on me. Look at me."

Slowly, he pointed the gun at his wife, his face betraying no emotion. "Put the gun on the floor or I'll shoot her."

"Herr Bohrmann . . ."

"I'll shoot her."

He was feeling calmer than ever before in his life, seized by a cold indifference that paralyzed his heart and darkened the sky. Franza saw it and knew she'd underestimated the danger.

"OK," she said. "OK, we want to stay calm now, don't we, Herr Bohrmann?"

Slowly, carefully, she pulled out the gun hidden in her waistband beneath the bulletproof vest. He watched her carefully.

"Put it on the floor," he said. "And kick it over to me."

She pushed her gun away with her foot, sending it sliding across the room. He walked over to it, picked it up, and threw it out into the hallway.

"I'm very tired," he said. "Very, very tired. Don't try to be a hero, you'll regret it."

He gave a little laugh, sweat running down his face, and he blinked and wiped his eyes with the back of his hand. She could hear and see his despair.

"Shouldn't we let your wife go?" she asked carefully. "It's getting late, noon already. Shouldn't she pick up the kids from kindergarten?"

"No," he said. "No. We won't let her go. And we won't let you go either! That's why I wanted you to come—so you'd stay, because all this shit is your fault."

"What do you mean, Herr Bohrmann? What's my fault? You have to help me out. Let's talk about it, tell me. We'll find a solution."

He laughed again. "How stupid do you think I am? There is no solution. Are you trying to lull me to sleep with your questions, with your sympathy? It's too late for that, you understand, too late! None of us will make it out of here alive, do you understand? Not you, not her, not me!"

He slumped a little, his voice breaking, but he held the gun steady and pointing at her. "Except for the children," he moaned quietly, "except for the children."

"Yes," Franza said. "The children. They need you. How many children do you have?"

She sensed him calm a bit. "Two," he said. "Lukas and Anja. They're at school. They're still little."

She nodded. "That's nice. You should enjoy this time, when they're still so little. It's a special time. Please, sit down."

She decided to talk about Ben. Bohrmann would listen, relax, soften.

Then a car came racing down the street. Franza and Bohrmann heard it at the same time: the screaming siren, the squealing tires, the loud voices. Probably the district attorney. He loved dramatic entrances.

Crap, Franza thought, *the moment has passed.*

And it had. Bohrmann tensed up and started waving the gun wildly in front of the two women. Franza was afraid he'd lose control completely if she didn't somehow manage to stop him.

"You think you can trick me! But it won't work!"

"Calm down!" Franza said, raising her hands. "Calm down. Don't lose control of yourself. You wanted to tell me what happened."

"The truth!" he said. "The truth happened! Don't you remember? You said so yourself: 'The truth is always the best way out.' Always! I believed you! Do you understand? I believed you! But the truth isn't the best way! For anyone! No one can bear the truth."

"What truth?" Franza asked, trying to remember exactly what she'd said that morning on the autobahn. She couldn't.

"My girlfriend left me," Bohrmann cried, sniffling and struggling to breathe. "She just took off. Things were too complicated for her."

He waved the gun around again, pointing it first at his wife, then at Franza. His wife sobbed, tugging in panic on the ropes around her wrists.

He pointed the gun at his wife again. "It's her fault that Nicole left me!" Bohrmann yelled. "It's your fault, bitch! That's why I'm going to shoot you now!"

He held out his arm with the gun, and Franza lunged toward him. *Where was the SWAT team? They should have taken the house right away,* she thought angrily, *right away, then it wouldn't have come to this.*

"Jens!" she shouted, hoping he'd hear her, hoping she'd get through to him somehow. "Jens, no! Don't do it! Calm down! Please, let's keep talking!"

It worked. It actually worked.

He closed his eyes for a brief moment, and then lowered the gun. "All right," he said. "Let's talk. Let's keep talking."

He slid down the wall onto the floor, wiped his forehead with his shirt sleeve, and said, "Go on, then, talk. Let's hear your words of wisdom. You must have some, you awesome policewoman."

Franza held out her hand. "Give me your gun, Jens. Nothing's happened yet. We can still fix this."

He was shaking his head and crying, the tears streaming down his face.

"The gun, Jens. Give me the gun," Franza said again. "End this now."

He shook his head again like a stubborn child. "No!" he said. "Stay away! I'll hurt you! Stay away from me."

"Oh, Jens."

"What was your name again?" he asked. "Some strange name, isn't it?"

"Franza," she said. "My name's Franza. Short for Franziska."

"Oh!" he said, laughing. "Short for Franziska."

"Yes," she said. "Exactly. I don't like it either. But we can't choose our own names."

He stopped laughing as suddenly as he'd started, and his face fell. "No," he said, "and we can't choose our lives."

Franza noted his change in mood.

"Especially not our lives! So what the hell are you talking about, Franza! I'll tell you something: I don't sleep anymore. Ever since that goddamned night I can't sleep. I keep seeing her coming toward me, in slow motion, and every time I think it'll pass. But it'll never be over, never! And I keep hearing the thud, Franza. I hear the thud, and it sounds like . . . I don't know what . . . and then she's flying through the air."

A shudder ran through him.

"You were as cold as ice when you got there, and you said: 'The truth is always the best way out.' And then you just took off and left me standing there with the so-called truth. But the fucking truth is: I killed somebody! That stupid bitch ran in front of my car and wrecked everything! Everything! Everything's turning to shit. Only she, over there—my wife—she doesn't get it. She doesn't understand it."

His voice dropped to a whisper now. Soon Jens Bohrmann would be running out of steam. Franza saw it, hoped for it, but it wasn't happening quite yet. She kneeled down in front of him, to look him in the eyes.

"I told her the truth," he whispered. "That woman—my wife—I told her the truth. Don't move, Franza! I told her I wasn't at the airport in Munich, that I hadn't been to Hamburg for work. Don't move, Franza! I told her that she pisses me off, that she's been pissing me off for so long. That I want to leave her! Don't move, Franza, stay where you are! I told you, I'll hurt you."

She looked at him and knew he meant it. She felt the coldness in his desperation and wondered what she'd done wrong, what she'd said, and what she shouldn't have said. She couldn't think of anything. He started to talk again in a flat, husky whisper. With his arm outstretched and the pistol ready he whispered his truth right in her face.

"Do you know what she said, Franza? Do you know what she said? That she loves me. She loves me anyway. She forgives me. Then she called Nicole on the phone and told her the same thing. That she loves me and forgives me and that she's there for me, especially now that it's so hard for me on account of the . . . accident. And then . . . the picture in the newspaper. I can't sleep anymore, every single night it's the same, no sleep. I just wander around from room to room. I drink to stop thinking—but I think anyway. Always the same thing, over and over."

He stood up and wiped his face. He was still crying.

"The accident wasn't your fault," Franza said as she slowly stood up next to him. "You didn't have a chance. Someone had already hurt the girl. She was injured and confused, that's why she ran in front of your car. You didn't have a chance—just like her."

His face contorted into a grotesque sneer. "Nice of you to say that, Franza. Wasn't her name Marie?"

Franza nodded.

"A beautiful name, Marie." He started to shake and wiped his face again. "It's over with Nicole. Too complicated she said, too complicated."

His teeth were chattering now. "But I love her," he said. "I love her."

"Listen, Jens," Franza said softly. "I'll talk to her. We'll find a solution."

"You think?" He smiled. "And how about her over there, Juliane?"

He pointed the gun at his wife. "Will we find a solution for her, too? So she'll leave me alone?"

He leaned closer to Franza and added in a conspiratorial whisper, "She's suffocating me, you understand? I can't breathe, I'm suffocating."

He turned around and looked at his wife, breathing heavily. Then he turned back to Franza and spoke so quietly she could barely hear.

"Even now," he whispered. "Even now, knowing I . . . cheated on her, knowing I want to leave her, knowing I don't love her anymore. She still won't let me go. Not even now. That's why I have to get rid of her. I've got to. So Nicole comes back, so I can sleep again. I have to get rid of her. Can I? Is it OK?"

Franza shook her head, slowly and deliberately.

His eyes were questioning, and he lowered his arm. "No, Franza? I shouldn't?"

Franza took a slow, deep breath. "No," she said softly. "No, you can't." She held out her hand to him. "I don't think so."

Then all of a sudden his wife broke out in a loud sob.

"But we vowed . . ." she sobbed. "We were . . . Jens! In the church, don't you remember? Till death do us part!"

Her voice got louder. *No,* Franza thought, *no!* Her heart nearly stopped.

"Yes," Bohrmann answered. "Yes, exactly."

Then he lifted his arm. And pulled the trigger.

It was so fast. Like a thought. Like a heartbeat.

The shot echoed through the house, through Franza's entire being, and there was nothing anyone could do.

Franza stood there paralyzed, feeling like she'd turned to ice—a lifeless lump. Juliane's mouth was open, but no sound came out. Her head sank onto her chest, her body went limp, and a dark stain spread quickly over her shirt. Franza thought of her eyes. Someone would have to close them because they never managed to do it themselves in time. There were always more eyes to close: brown hazelnuts or green apples.

Then the SWAT team was there. Shouting, crashing. Bohrmann was disarmed and thrown to the ground, his hands bound behind him.

Felix was there, too, gauging the situation and wrapping his arms around Franza. Major Andresy entered the room, checked the woman's vital signs, and said: "Dead. We'll have to call Borger."

They went outside.

A distant melody in the sky, somewhere among the heavens. Franza breathed in deeply. It faded.

"I was worried about you," Felix said.

She didn't say anything, still breathing deeply.

Bohrmann was led past them by two policemen—in handcuffs, abrasions on his face and arms. He'd seemed taller before. Now he was broken and wouldn't heal. He stopped. "I screwed up," he said. "Didn't I?"

Franza nodded.

"The children," he said. "Will you make sure . . . ?"

She nodded.

"Will you visit me?" he asked.

"No," she said. "No."

He nodded. Then they led him away.

The children stood on the sidewalk like creatures from another planet, too little for this moment and too little for what was to come. Their aunt, Juliane's sister, had picked them up from kindergarten at noon. Jens had called her in the morning and told her he and Juliane had an appointment with a marriage counselor. A crisis intervention team was taking care of the children now, shielding them from what was happening. They were in good hands, but were they going to be good enough for what was ahead?

The district attorney came over, furious. "Oberwieser!" he fumed. "Why didn't you call social services right after the accident? This man's mental condition must have been obvious!"

She shook her head and felt exhaustion creeping through her veins like heavy, ancient magma. Her bones felt like lead.

"I didn't see any reason to," she said. "I didn't think it was necessary."

"Well, you were wrong," he said coolly. "There'll be consequences."

Asshole, she thought. *You arrogant asshole, what do you know?*

32

She'd asked for a half-hour break. She was sitting in the courtyard of a cafe looking out into the sunlight, feeling outcast and illegitimate, at the mercy of the anarchy in her head.

The wind passed softly over the oleander bushes between the courtyard and the parking lot. The sun shone through the luscious tops, creating quivering, fluttering shadows on the ground, as if oleander leaves had wings, as if they were flying out into the bright expanse of the universe.

She thought of Arthur's ashen face when she came out of the house, of the patches of sweat on his shirt, of his deep sigh of relief—whereas the district attorney . . .

She pushed the cold cappuccino away, put a few coins on the table, and left.

So now there were two bodies. And Brückl, the district attorney, who was a theatrical person and loved dramatic scenes, was possibly right.

Should she have called social services after the girl stumbled out in front of Bohrmann's car, destroying not only her own life, but Bohrmann's as well? How could she have known that his life was so messed up, that death was the only way out for him?

How could she have known he'd go to pieces?

Men left their wives. Mothers left their children. In a city like New York sirens were going off all the time. In a town like this the fog crept up from the Danube, covering everything—at least from time to time.

Franza thought of Bohrmann's wife, Juliane.

She'd loved her husband in a way that was dangerous, dangerous because it was closer to death than to life. She was connected to him symbiotically, so symbiotically that there was no escape. They were caught in this web like a spider's prey—they were each prey and spider at the same time. Franza now understood that they didn't have a chance. There was no way out, nothing.

Felix was at the curb leaning against his car, doors wide open. The heat was stifling. *Lead,* she thought, *bones of lead. When will I fall apart?*

"I think she wanted to die," she said on their way back to the office. "She knew what she had to say for him to shoot her. And she said it."

Felix looked at her with surprise. "Why?"

She didn't have to think about it. "Because he didn't love her anymore," she said. "And she was nothing without his love."

"You think?" Felix asked. "Don't you think that's a little far-fetched? A little dramatic?"

Franza shook her head. "No," she said. "That's how it was."

They fell silent. Franza thought about what Port had said earlier—only a few hours ago, yet it felt like an eternity. About making a choice, about choosing in a fraction of a second. Choosing life or death. And how quick it was to turn from life to death.

Felix got into the turning lane, the traffic backing up a long way in the heat. There'd be a few people losing it today.

"And the children?" Felix asked.

Franza shrugged helplessly.

"Sad," Felix said. "Very sad. What sort of a job are we in?"

Franza attempted a smile. "We're looking for the truth," she said. "We'll find it. Someone has to."

33

They stood in the hallway venting their anger and grief. Young women—girls, really. There were five of them left. One of their group had been killed, and they would never forgive whoever was responsible. One wouldn't come back, and the rest were angry and grief-stricken.

Their leader was a tall woman with a bright, alert face and dark circles around her eyes. The others formed the wall.

They wanted to be impenetrable, just like a wall, silent to the end—the detectives could see that right away. But what they knew might be essential.

They'd be hard to crack, Franza knew. They'd try to sort it out themselves, even if it put them in danger. Danger wasn't new to them; they'd dealt with it all their lives, sometimes it had been unavoidable, and that's why they were here, stranded in this supposed safe haven.

They were standing in the hallway, silent, wearing dark pants and jackets. It was as if light and colors no longer existed, only their faces glowed bright in the darkness, letting their vulnerability show if you looked closely—if you *knew* how to look closely. Then in those eyes with the dark circles around them, you could see the vulnerability, how they had been hurt again and again. They knew what it was like when the pain flared up and burned them. They knew its permanence—its persistence—and that's why they'd fight it to the last. That's why they were forming a wall that was impenetrable to the pain—unlike the anger, which they let in. The anger gave them strength for revenge and punishment, strength to punish the person responsible.

Erinyes, Franza thought and shuddered, *furies, goddesses of vengeance.*

Wham, Felix thought, *they'd just shoot you down if you were in the way. Maybe I should duck?*

34

They had driven out to one of the suburbs. Marie had lived in a high-rise building where two apartments were connected to accommodate six young women. Supported by social workers, the women were trying to get their lives together.

"Come in," said Martha Hauer, the social worker. She led them into the living room.

"It'll be tricky with them," she said, sitting down at the wobbly table. "As you just saw."

Franza nodded, then took a quick look around the room. It exuded as much charm as a high-school common room. The furniture was cheap and worn-out, there were stains on the couch, and nothing matched.

"Well," the social worker said as if she'd read Franza's mind. "There's never enough money, just like everywhere. But we try."

She sighed, pausing for a moment. "Can you tell me what happened to Marie?"

Felix cleared his throat. "We don't know very much yet. We're still learning about her life—and we need your help for that. You were something like her family, weren't you?"

The woman thought for a moment, giving a short, sad laugh. "Her family. Yes, if you want to call it that. It didn't help her, though. I wonder . . ."

She paused again and shook her head while holding it in her hands and covering her face. When she looked back up she'd pulled herself together again. "What a horrible thing to happen. She was doing so well and now this!"

She shook her head again, took off her glasses, and cleaned them with a tissue. "You have no idea," she said, "all the things our girls have been through."

Franza shrugged. "Oh, you know," she said, "I think our jobs are more closely related than you think. What are you trying to achieve here?"

"We're a social institution for girls between seventeen and twenty-one. We help them gain independence, try to teach them how to live, you might say. How to live a normal life: manage finances, find employment, finish school—friendships, love, contraception, having children. Right here in the middle of this mess—a Sisyphean task, believe me."

She nodded as if to lend weight to her words. Franza nodded, too. *What's her problem,* she thought, feeling agitation building inside her. *Is she a saint or something? Don't we all have Sisyphean tasks?*

Anger rumbled and raged inside her, like a fist squeezing her and taking her breath away. *Well,* she thought mockingly, *you holy woman of Sisyphusland, can you carry your burden?*

The woman nodded again. *Is she a mind reader,* Franza wondered, *do you learn that, too, in your oh-so-empathetic job?*

"Most of all, we try to get them out of the vicious circle of violence many are trapped in."

Of course, what a surprise! How unexpected.

The fist in Franza's stomach clenched tighter and tighter. "And does it work?"

Franza felt Felix's surprised eyes on her. She didn't know herself why she was feeling so aggressive all of a sudden. Maybe it was time to admit that the day's events had shaken her more than she wanted to believe.

The social worker grimaced, and tilted her head to one side. "Not always," she said then with pointed friendliness. "Do you solve all your cases?"

Felix had to grin a little. "No," he said, "unfortunately not. But let's focus on Marie again, shall we?"

"Of course," the woman said. "But I haven't even offered you anything—coffee?" She got up.

When they'd finally settled down in front of steaming cups of coffee and cheap supermarket cookies, which Franza—unlike Felix—wouldn't touch, they finally talked about Marie. She'd been through all kinds of state homes before landing in this residential group, which called itself WINGS.

What a crappy name, Felix thought, *a spectacularly poor choice.* "Interesting name," he said, feeling Franza's hostile gaze. "How did you think of that?"

"Yes, isn't it?" Hauer said with a shy smile. Happiness showed in her face, which turned pink and began to glow. "Well, I don't even remember. It just came to us. We wanted a name full of hope, and wings . . . flying . . . that seemed like the epitome of hope."

Felix smiled and nodded politely, then returned to their subject of interest. "Marie?"

The social worker sighed. "Yes, Marie."

Marie, who kept running away from home. Who hung around in parks night after night, slept in train stations and shelters. Marie, who was incapable of thinking straight or feeling, lost in the buzz of the pills and the urge to cut herself. The cutting eased the pressure; the pain broke the heaviness of life into tufts of cotton candy.

Your wings, Franza thought, *you really broke your wings, my darling. A fitting name, really.*

"Tell us about the other girls," she said. "Why are they here?"

The social worker looked into her cup and gave a sad laugh. "The usual," she said. "Broken families, abuse, drugs, whatever you like. Pick one; I've got everything to offer you. But I'm guessing you know that, since our jobs are so closely related, as you kindly pointed out."

She looked up and waited for a moment. When she continued, the irony had left her voice. "Families with alcohol abuse, often unemployed and lower class, no one wants them, so they lash out in anger and desperation. I know that's no excuse, but that's just the way it is. Most of the time it's the girls copping out because they're the weakest, defenseless. The beatings are the least of their worries: many have to fear for their lives; many end up on the street as prostitutes. Very few manage to break out of it."

She fell silent again and looked out the window. "They get their daughters high on drugs and porn, and then take them to bed with them. Their sons, too. It's probably not even that difficult. Children don't put up a fight, and how could they? They're scared and don't know anything different."

She took a deep breath, nodding emphatically. "That's what it's like in this beautiful country of ours. And actually it happens in all social classes. But that isn't anything new to you."

She turned her head to look out the window again. She'd become cynical over the years, disheartened. She'd seen too much and failed too often. Idealism? What's that?

"In my job," she said, turning back to the detectives, "you develop a pretty thick skin, just like in your job. You've got to, I guess, but some things . . . some things still get under your skin. That's why most of my colleagues don't last very long. Four or five years, then they look for another job."

She nodded toward the door. "Jennifer out there, the tall one with all the black around her eyes. Her father was drunk and stabbed her mother to death while Jenny watched. She was eleven. She grabbed her little sister Jessica and hid in the cellar for two days. When the police finally found them, Jenny stepped in front of her sister, holding a pocketknife to protect her. They had a hard time getting it away from her."

Yes, Franza thought, *you're right, of course. But we all know these stories.* She stood up and went to the window. The sun beat down on the road.

"If something isn't going her way," the social worker continued, "she lashes out. As quick as lightning, without warning, bam! Theoretically she shouldn't be here anymore. Violence isn't tolerated, that's our first rule. No violence, no alcohol, no drugs, no prostitution. But where do you think she'll end up if we kick her out?"

She paused again briefly. "She's scared of the dark, needs the light on to go to sleep. Isn't it funny?"

No, Franza thought, *not funny.* She looked out the window, but all she could see were the neighboring buildings. There were no wide-open spaces, no ocean, no sky.

"And Cosima, the short blonde. Her father is a musician, her mother a doctor. They had high hopes for her: English-speaking kindergarten, ballet, piano lessons, prestigious school, university, you know, the works. The world at her feet, the high life. But Cosima didn't cooperate, simply didn't work out like they wanted her to. She failed at school, took up smoking pot, got stoned and was caught by the police, totaled the family car. Just little things like that, so they kicked her out, Herr and Frau Doctor. At fifteen."

"You can't save them all," Franza said a little too loud, meaning herself.

The social worker laughed her strange little laugh. "Yes, that's true. As we can see with Marie."

She refilled their cups. "Marie was on her way to becoming a success story, probably our only one. All of a sudden she started going back to school, aced her finals, and planned to go to Berlin to study. She would have received a scholarship, and we already had arranged a room for her in the dormitory. She would have made it."

Pride was evident in her voice. She was in her early forties and her body was gaunt and showing signs of stiffness, though her graying hair probably made her look older than she was.

And how about me, Franza thought, alarmed, *how old do I look?*

"What was she going to study?" Felix asked, glancing anxiously at Franza. *Why does he look so worried?* she thought. *What does he think I'll do, silly man?*

"She wanted to be an actress and had signed up to take the entrance exam at a university. I'm sure she would have made it."

The pride was back in the social worker's voice, and the soft pink color returned to her face. It showed in her sparkling eyes, and at that moment she looked beautiful. Then the regret and melancholy returned.

Franza raised her eyebrows. *To Berlin to be an actress, I see.*

"Did she have a boyfriend?"

"No. No . . . boyfriend. Not as far as I know." Felix heard the hesitation in her voice.

"But she was in love. That's what she wrote her mother. Are you sure you don't know anything about it?"

The social worker thought for a moment, moving her head from side to side. "Maybe," she said. "Maybe you're right; there may have been someone in the last few weeks. She was . . . different. Softer, hopeful, happy. The girls noticed, too, and teased her about it. But it didn't bother her, she seemed . . . very certain."

Franza saw the tenderness in her eyes again, and it touched her.

"And?" Felix asked impatiently.

She shook her head regretfully. "Nothing. I don't know any more. She didn't talk about herself very much. When I asked her how she was doing, she said fine, and that she was confident she'd make it. But then . . . something must have gone wrong."

"Dr. Lauberts—does the name ring a bell?"

"Yes, of course." She didn't seem surprised.

"You're not surprised we're asking about him?"

She shrugged, looking very tired all of a sudden. "I've wondered about that for some time."

Felix nodded. "Great. So what do you know?"

She hesitated briefly. "I'm guessing she was involved with him somehow. Or rather, he with her."

Franza came back to the table and sat down. "He paid her. I assume you know what that's called."

"Yes," the social worker said softly. "Of course I know what that's called."

"Could Lauberts be Marie's murderer?"

Startled, Hauer looked up and frowned. "Do you believe so?"

"We don't believe anything. We investigate. We look at all the angles. What do you believe?"

She shrugged. "I don't know, either," she said. "No, I can't imagine it, not really. But then again I couldn't imagine that he of all people . . ."

She fell silent, looking down.

"What? Frau Hauer?"

"Would turn her into a hooker," she said reluctantly. Suddenly she had tears in her eyes, and she quickly turned away, trying to hide them.

The detectives looked at her with surprise and renewed interest. Was it possible . . . ? Could it be . . . ? Was there any chance of that . . . ?

"Why didn't you do anything about this . . . relationship?"

She looked down at the tablecloth and flicked some crumbs to the floor. "I've only known about it myself for two weeks, since this strange visit of his . . . I'm guessing you've heard about it. Our intern told me, of course. I confronted Marie, but she only laughed at me."

"And?"

She shook her head, bewildered. "And what?"

"Do you know of any other . . . clients?"

She gave a short laugh and brushed hair out of her face. "What are you talking about?"

"Apparently there's a list, and we'd like to have it. Do you know anything?"

"No, how should I?"

"Don't you have a certain legal responsibility?"

Hauer sighed and looked impatient. "Do you always know what your children are doing?"

That hit home.

One–nothing, your favor, Franza thought, picturing Ben.

Touché, Felix thought, picturing Marlene.

But Franza wasn't ready to give up just yet. "Tell me again—what were your guidelines?"

They could see in her eyes how tired the social worker was, how fed up she was with all of it. *Lead,* Franza thought, *in your bones, everywhere. I know how it feels.*

"Listen," Frau Hauer said. "I've been working in this job forever, way too long, probably. Just like you maybe. If we'd met in different circumstances, we might even have been friends."

I don't think so, Franza thought, *I really don't. I don't like you self-proclaimed Samaritans, you do-gooders.*

It's possible, Felix thought indifferently, *perhaps.*

The social worker paused for a moment, taking a deep breath. "What I'm trying to say is, I did the best I could for Marie, and you just have to believe that. I was sure she'd make it, clean break and everything. She was doing so well!"

She shook her head. "But time and time again I get blindsided by the fact that anything is possible, that there is a dark side . . . and that's why . . . besides, she was over twenty."

Franza opened her mouth. She was about to say, *Let's get back to Lauberts . . . Could it be that you and he . . . and that's what's holding you back?*

But she didn't say anything and just looked at Felix, who was tugging at her sleeve. "Leave it alone," he muttered.

Aha, she thought, *gotcha. That really hit home. All right, I'm tired, too. Let's leave it for now. Let's do it some other time, poor woman.*

She turned away, and Felix continued.

"The girls, would they know anything?"

She shrugged. "Maybe, but I don't think so. She was a loner, preferred being by herself."

"We'll interview them anyway, individually."

"If you think it'll help."

The social worker leaned back and folded her arms. "Jennifer and Marie sometimes spent time together. If anyone knows anything about Marie's"—she paused for a moment—"private life, it'd be Jenny. But I'm certain you won't get a word out of her."

"Why? Why would she want Marie's death to remain unpunished, with her murderer running around loose?"

"He won't."

Felix rolled his eyes inwardly, but Franza asked patiently, "What do you mean?"

Martha Hauer brought her fingertips together and stared into her empty cup. "It's simple," she said. "'They'll take care of him themselves."

35

Interviewing the girls was just as fruitless as the social worker had predicted. They listened to the questions in silence, staring blankly into thin air.

"Let's drop it," Felix said. "We're not getting anywhere. Time to give it up—for now anyway."

Martha Hauer excused herself. "You're all right on your own here? I've got an appointment. If you have any questions . . ."

She gestured toward the young woman who'd arrived a short time ago. She nodded at them from the kitchen.

"Thank you," Franza said, examining Hauer's tanned arms and face. Tennis-court tan? Playing with Lauberts?

"We might have more questions for you," Franza said. "We won't hesitate to contact you again."

The social worker parried the ironic tone of voice with a strange, sad smile. "I assumed so."

Franza watched through the window until Hauer walked down the street, got into a car, and drove off. "I bet," she said, feeling a faint tingling, "I bet Marie—the naughty girl—stole her lover."

Was this a lead? Just a small one, maybe?

She turned around to look at Felix. "Yes," he said as he pulled his cell phone from his jacket. "I'm afraid you're right."

"Arthur," he said, "I have two names for you. I want to know everything, both private life and professional—especially private. We suspect our girl interfered with someone's love life. But be discreet. All right?"

Franza nodded, satisfied. "Let's take a look at her room," she suggested. "Before we send the forensic people."

Marie's bedroom was completely different from the one at her mother's house. No little girl's room like that one. There was nothing childish about this room. It was plain and convenient. The furniture was as motley as that in the living room. There was a bed, a desk, a wardrobe, and a bookshelf containing a surprisingly large number of books. Exercise books, textbooks, and folders were stacked on the desk along with pencils, pens, and paper.

Obviously Marie hadn't gotten around to tidying up, to sorting and throwing things out from her last term. Now it was too late.

Franza sighed thinking about how much Ben had enjoyed going through his school things last year and making a huge bonfire out in the yard with all the books and papers he never wanted to see again. It had been cathartic—for him and for Franza and Max. For weeks after they'd had to pick up the charred remains of paper and ashes from all over their yard.

Franza walked over to the desk and wistfully leafed through the books and folders. Would they discover Marie's secrets here, perhaps even the ominous list they weren't even sure existed?

Felix interrupted her train of thought. "The visitors' record," he said, "we haven't even looked at it. Maybe we'll find other interesting names in it. I'll go have a look and ask the young lady out there a few questions." He left, closing the door behind him.

Franza walked over to the bed and carefully sat down on the edge. As always, it felt like a desecration.

The corner of a shirt was peeping out from under the blanket, a pajama top perhaps, and she pulled it out and held it up. It was a big T-shirt with Winnie the Pooh and Piglet on the front. Franza smiled. What a surprise! Winnie the Pooh here in Marie's bed.

Had he given back to her a tiny piece of the childhood she'd lost so early? A faint feeling of warmth, of safety, at least? Franza hoped so.

Ben had loved him, too, Pooh. Back when they were still allowed to call him Benny or Benjamin. He'd owned everything that could be bought of Winnie the Pooh and his friends: bedding, jerseys, backpack, water bottle, coloring books, comic books, picture books. And, of course, the whole gang of stuffed animals.

The little bear had sat in the corner of his bed for years, and one day Benny, in a serious mood, had scribbled his name on its little red shirt with a permanent marker. That way, he'd reasoned, if someone took his bear away from him he'd have an easier time finding it.

Franza smiled, looked at Pooh's face, and slowly put the T-shirt back on the bed. What had happened to Ben's treasures?

She tried to remember when she'd put them away and where, but she couldn't remember. Had Ben put them away himself? Somewhere in the depths of his drawers and wardrobe? So that no one could take them away from him, ever?

Wistfully, she attempted a laugh. Where had those times gone? And that place where they'd been so happy—Benny, Max, and herself? Had that place even really existed, and those times? For more than a few precious moments?

And where the hell was he now, Ben? Why couldn't she get hold of him?

Yes, OK, it was true he always lost his phones—he was on his fifth or sixth one now—but was that really all there was to it?

Why couldn't she shake this weird feeling she'd had the last few days? That something had happened. Something dangerous. Something that would blow them away.

Bullshit, she thought, and repeated it out loud. *"Just bullshit! I'm getting worked up over nothing."*

She folded the T-shirt carefully and got up. *I have to stay focused,* she thought, shaking her head vigorously. *I can't keep drifting off into my personal problems, imagining horrible scenarios for no reason!*

She took a deep breath, trying to calm herself—without success. Somewhere deep inside her head she could feel a migraine coming on, rising toward her like glowing lava. *No,* she thought, *not now, please. Don't come stalking now, tiger, sleep on, stay down!*

She folded the blanket back to put the T-shirt underneath, and then she saw it.

36

Afterward, she could barely remember how she'd gotten out of the apartment. Panic had driven her, and fear, she remembered. She had vague memories of the surprised expressions on the girls' faces, and of Felix's voice as he called out to her, and that he rushed out the door after her.

But by then she was already getting into the car, keys in hand. They'd done it like this for years. Each had their own set of car keys so they could act fast and independently in precarious situations. Was this a precarious situation?

He'd be asking himself this question, Felix. Franza knew he'd be asking himself other things, too, but she couldn't worry about that right now.

She put her foot down on the gas and shot out of the parking spot with squealing tires as if she'd lost her mind, ignoring the driver coming from behind her who'd had to slam on his brakes, cursing and honking. But she didn't care; she'd forgotten before she turned into the next side street.

When her cell phone rang, she turned it off and threw it on the backseat. She knew it could only be Felix, and she knew she couldn't talk to him right then, not while she was still processing this damned realization that had scared her to death.

Ben and Marie. Marie and Ben. Over and over. Ben and Marie. Marie and Ben.

Franza's thoughts were spinning around and around. Ben and Marie, Marie and Ben. What did they have to do with each other? What was Ben doing in her murder investigation? How could he just come barging in without notice, without warning, taking over her every thought and feeling?

It had pierced her heart like a needle, taking away her breath and showing her what fear was, real fear, mortal fear. Winnie the Pooh, the cutest of all bears, was innocently sleeping underneath Marie's blanket, wedged between the mattress and the wall. Pooh, with Ben's name scribbled on the tiny red shirt with brutal finality, leaving an undeniable message. BENNY in scrawled letters on the bear's red shirt in Marie's bed, this damned stuffed toy she hadn't seen in years and whose existence she'd almost forgotten.

And now! It turned up here . . .

Like a fist in her stomach, a blow to her head. Franza swallowed back the urge to retch.

. . . in this room, the animal under the girl's bedcovers. What the hell did that mean, what?

Was Ben the mysterious stranger, the boy Marie had been in love with but no one knew and no one had seen? More like a shadow, a ghost in the fog?

What did the social worker say? That she'd been different in the last few weeks. Softer, hopeful and confident that she'd make it in her new life.

So was it Ben who'd changed her like this and made her happy?

Was it also he who . . . killed her in the end?

Because something had gone wrong, as the social worker put it?

Was this the reason he wasn't answering their calls, because this love story had ended so terribly, so unforeseeably terribly?

Was he on the run—running away from himself, from despair, and ultimately from her, Franza, his mother, whose job is to investigate and solve mysteries and find answers?

No, it can't be! This just can't be, Franza thought as she raced wildly through town toward the autobahn. *Can my worst fears be coming true?*

Maybe she was just being hysterical and she had it all wrong. Only half an hour ago she'd suspected Hauer, the social worker with the unhappy love and sex life. Wasn't it still possible she'd been overzealous in getting rid of Marie?

How quickly everything can change! Just when everything seemed clear, all it took was for something tiny to change, and everything was different.

This time, however, it wasn't just a tiny clue, but a solid piece of evidence.

But evidence of what?

Really, only of the fact that Ben and Marie had known each other, not even that they'd been in love. That's all. But why the hell wasn't he calling her back if he had nothing to hide?

"Ben!" she shouted. "Damn it! Why aren't you calling?"

She took the autobahn heading toward Berlin, speeding along mile after mile in a daze, at times struggling to keep the car under control when she had to brake hard because the idiots around her hadn't learned how to drive. A strange euphoria came over her. *So what,* she thought, *if I roll over, then I'll be gone, then it'll be over, and then peace, forever.*

But she was a good driver. She was trained on police test tracks and always excelled in crash tests and simulated car chases. She was ready for anything and prepared for the ultimate situation X, requiring nerves of steel. She always had them, was proud of them. But now her nerves of steel had disintegrated, dissolved— melted away like snow on a warm spring day.

The rest area where Marie was killed came into view. As Franza put on her turn signal, turned off the road, and let the car roll to a halt, she felt a sudden wave rising up inside her. She jumped out of the car in panic, ran to the curb, and vomited convulsively until nothing came out but clear mucus and green bile.

A man came to her aid. She could only see him through a blurry veil, like a ghost, but she had a vague feeling she knew him. He must have come from one of the cars or from the restrooms. He grabbed her shoulders, but she shook him off, holding up her arms defensively.

"It's all right," she gasped, "I'm fine. I'll be all right in a moment."

But she wasn't all right. She could feel the fist in her stomach again, and the convulsions returned.

This time she let the man brush her hair out of her face while she emptied her stomach down to the last drop of mucus. Then she began to shake. Her teeth chattered, and all the color drained from her face. She struggled for breath. Her heart seemed to stop, and she thought she was dying. She could see Bohrmann in his last few moments of hesitation, saw him pointing his gun at her and then at his wife, heard Juliane's scream filling her head and grabbing hold of her brain. Then the shot went off, and it felt as if it ricocheted right through her while Juliane screamed and screamed and slumped forward, and suddenly it was Ben who'd fired the shot, and she herself slumped forward, screaming and feeling the pain raging deep inside her, ripping her apart, and it was Ben's bullet that caromed through her body, killing her. And finally, there was silence.

"Sit down," the man said and led her to a bench. "Come now, sit down. You're a mess. I'll go get you some water."

Still shaking, she lay down on the bench, curled up on her side, hoping the silence would stay with her, silence in her head and her body and everywhere.

She knew the man had returned when he put his hand on her head and stroked her hair gently. *Nice,* she thought, *how nice. I want to die.*

His smell seemed familiar to her—she'd smelled it somewhere not long ago. She remembered because she'd liked it, but she couldn't think from when and where she knew it.

"I want to die," she said and enjoyed the darkness and silence behind her closed eyelids. "Now, right now, on the spot. Please let me," she said, "let me die."

He kept stroking her hair, and his touch was cool and damp because he was dribbling water onto her forehead while standing hunched over right behind her. She could feel his face close to hers, but couldn't see it.

"No," he said, and something in his voice didn't allow for contradiction. "You won't die. It doesn't go that fast."

"How do you know?" she whispered into the blackness of her eyelids. "Nobody can know that."

"Yes," he said. "Yes, I know."

37

She was so soft, *Ben thought,* so incredibly soft sleeping in my arms. *He would watch the pulse in her neck while she slept. He'd softly put a finger on the spot so he could feel her heartbeat, thump, thump, thump, when she was asleep after having kissed and slept with him—after his pants had gotten tight because his cock was aching for her.*

"*That's perfectly normal,*" *she'd said, laughing and sliding her hand between his legs, which hadn't helped things at all.*

"*Don't be embarrassed. That's perfectly normal for people with penises,*" *she'd laughed.* "*And you're a proven penis person, as we both know, aren't you?*"

He'd had to laugh, too, and he missed that now that she was gone, the laughing together, a mingling of high and low and middle sounds, like a sonata, like a sonata by Mozart or Beethoven or whomever.

This observation had made her laugh again. "*Aren't you the artistic one?!*" *she'd said.* "*Did your mom send you to music classes?*"

Her fingers danced across an invisible piano, and she skipped and bounced out into the sunshine on the meadow wet with dew, her feet leaving prints in the grass, which he followed like a faithful puppy, and then they rolled down a bank and into each other's arms and made love.

He'd trembled against her, breathless, the tip of her tongue on his body, his hands on hers. She moved her hair in the wind that smelled of summer, of the Sahara, and of the hay drying in the meadows, and her eyes shone like hazelnuts in oil.

We never had the autumn, *Ben thought,* and hardly any summer. "See you soon," she'd said and smiled. Then she hadn't come back.

Poppies and elderflowers along the river, the shimmering water. They'd had the silence, the wind, the trees, and the clarity that came from their hearts. He thought of her touch, and his cock hardened with the memory, her touch was like foam on the dark river waters.

That's how it had been, he could swear to it. Not like a good-bye from the start.

38

Felix had called Arthur. Get his ass in gear and pick him up—preferably yesterday. Forget everything he'd been told to do earlier. Danger was imminent. Don't ask what or why, discretion was the order of the day, discretion toward everyone and everything. In short: switch off brain, shut mouth, get a move on. Felix was counting on him.

Arthur complied enthusiastically, confirming once again they'd made the right decision in taking him on.

While he waited, Felix checked through the visitors' record, but there were no surprises. Franza's running away—he didn't know what else to call it—had confused him. Eventually he confronted the young woman on duty with the fact that Marie had been prostituting herself, and asked if she knew anything about it. She knew nothing, but seemed surprised and possibly shocked. As usual, Felix struggled to tell the difference between these slightly different shades of emotion.

Arthur finally showed up, and they drove back to town. Felix cursed loudly. Franza still wasn't answering her phone. He couldn't get hold of Max either, and the actor had an unlisted number, which the bastard at directory assistance wouldn't give him, because, he said, anyone could call and say they're police and it's life-or-death.

Felix was foaming at the mouth but couldn't counter this argument. Arthur seemed surprised when he heard the actor's name.

Eventually Felix gave up and focused instead on getting in touch with the contacts he'd carefully developed over his years as a policeman. If there was a police call or a medical emergency anywhere in town involving a woman around forty who even remotely resembled Franza, Felix would know right away.

And that's what happened.

The phone call came just as Felix and Arthur were pulling into the police station.

"A9 toward Berlin, outside Munich," said the ambulance driver with whom Felix occasionally played squash.

"Let me guess," Felix said. "The rest area between Lenting and Denkendorf."

"Bingo," the driver replied, clicking his tongue approvingly. "You're in the right job. Are you coming? Do you want us to wait? We're in no particular hurry."

Arthur had already turned the car around.

"What happened?"

"She collapsed, looks like she's in shock. Panic attack. This heat probably didn't help. She's much better already, though she probably shouldn't be driving."

"Who called you?"

"A Turkish guy who spoke in broken German. She was lying on a bench when we got here and a Turkish family was standing around her. They managed to explain that a man had asked them to call us and to keep an eye on her until we arrived. He took off. Bit strange if you ask me. I don't know anything else, though."

"Are they still there?"

"Who?"

"The family." He struggled to hide his impatience.

"No," the driver said. "They took off as soon as we got here. Why?"

"Did you happen to write down their license number so we can find them again?"

It was quiet on the other end for a moment, and Felix could practically feel the man's surprise through the phone. "No," he said slowly in the end. "Should I have? Why?"

"Never mind," Felix said lightly, but sighed to himself. "It's not so important, but I just would have liked a description of that man. Do you think my colleague will be able to describe him?"

Again, brief hesitation on the other end. "Well, as far as I can tell she was too busy falling down and throwing up to really get a good look. Sorry."

"OK," Felix said. "I kind of expected that. Can't help it, but thanks anyway. We'll be there in a few minutes. I owe you one; I'll let you win next time."

The ambulance driver laughed, but Felix didn't feel like laughing.

A man who didn't want to be recognized? At this rest area of all places? He'd have Arthur look around for cigarette butts.

39

He left. She would be in good hands. He had done everything he could, but he had to take off.

40

She didn't look as bad as he'd expected. She smiled bravely. "I'm sorry Felix," she said. "I can't explain right now. Maybe tomorrow."

He took her home.

Max was in the garden tending the grill. Felix immediately felt hungry and checked the time. It was late, past his dinnertime, and he hadn't even had lunch.

The men exchanged a jovial greeting. "Hungry?" Max asked. "There's plenty. Here you go, catch!"

He tossed him a bottle of beer, which Felix caught skillfully and opened on the edge of a side table.

"I'm going to bed," Franza said, surprised in some distant part of her brain that Max didn't seem at all jealous of Felix, but she soon forgot about it again. "I have to sleep."

She walked toward the house, feeling how exhaustion was turning her limbs to Play-Doh, like a doll without joints, and feeling Max's and Felix's eyes following her.

"This case," she heard Max whispering, "it's taking it out of you two, isn't it?"

"Yes," Felix replied. "You could say that."

She rested for a while on the bench by the door to the terrace. The food on the grill smelled divine. She felt how empty her stomach was, but she knew she still wouldn't be able to eat a thing.

"Have you heard from Ben?"

Max shook his head. "She's worried about her grown son," he said, looking at Felix. "Because he's on vacation, enjoying life and forgetting to call her."

He laughed. "Just look out when your kids are grown-up!"

Oh, Max, Franza thought, looking up, *you don't know anything.* The sky above was still blue, but the sunlight was not so strong.

"Until tomorrow," she said quietly to herself, stroking Winnie the Pooh in her bag. *How far,* she thought, *how far am I from going over the edge?*

In the shower, she tried to fill the gap in her memory. She didn't know exactly how large it was, but she felt the echo of an enormous fright, like icy breath on the back of her neck. Then there was the voice she thought she'd heard before, a smell, the shadow of a man, his face close to hers yet unrecognizable through the fog she had fallen into.

In the end, she hadn't died. In the end, she was back home, among all the familiar things that made up her life. They did not seem strange to her, even now when nothing else felt certain. It gave her a bit of hope that she could rely on some kind of permanence—there were symbols and rituals that stayed with her even when everything else was falling apart.

Out in the yard the men were talking soccer, predicting Sunday's game would be a disaster. Felix talked about his toothache and how Angelika wouldn't let him into bed if he ate too much garlic, and Max scolded him for not calling him sooner about the pain. Of course he'd fit him in the next day, whatever time suited him—and Angelika shouldn't make such a fuss.

Through the skylight Franza could see the light changing as night approached. A plane was leaving a vapor trail in the sky, smooth and straight at first, then fanning out and disappearing in the deep blue of dusk as Franza slipped into a restless sleep.

. . .

Three hours later, when Felix tiptoed into his own bedroom, Angelika was fast asleep. He carefully sat down on the edge of their bed and looked at her for a long time. She woke up, grumbled unintelligibly, and then turned over and asked, "Where have you been all this time?" Then she went back to sleep.

Soon there'd be seven of them. He began to feel just a tiny bit excited about these little ones who'd inexplicably decided to come as twins. "Don't be afraid," he said softly. "I'm here now."

As he listened to Angelika's regular breathing, he suddenly realized the pregnancy might have another positive.

Maybe, he hoped fervently, just maybe Angelika would finally agree to hire someone to help in the kitchen.

Just enough so that once or twice a week he'd get something edible, he thought, his excitement growing, maybe something scrumptious, something he could look forward to with every single taste bud.

Then I wouldn't mind even another child, a sixth one if she wanted, he thought. *I wouldn't care.*

He knew it was disloyal, but he couldn't help it. He loved her dearly, but her cooking was just awful.

The fancy, upscale meals she prepared every day spoiled his appetite before he even tried them. The meals were indefinable, but healthy, very healthy, she always assured him.

Thank God for Franza and the cookies she brought in every day. They gave him a satiated feeling, like Christmas all year round. It made his longing for his mother's solid farm-cooked meals easier to bear.

He thought of her wistfully, of her roasts and dumplings, stews and puddings, and her cakes and pies. Even after he'd left for the university in Frankfurt she spoiled him. Her care packages were legendary, and he'd celebrated huge feasts with his fellow students.

He gently tapped Angelika's belly, which was still as flat as a board, and asked for her forgiveness. He thought about how the world used to be big and he small, and how this had started to turn around sometime in the middle of his life.

Finally he stood up, undressed, and stepped into the cold shower. When he came back, Angelika had kicked off the sheets, and he covered her up again. "No!" she mumbled. "Don't! It's too hot." When he tried to snuggle up to her romantically, she said it again.

He knew it was a punishment, and accepted it humbly. Then he dreamed of roast duck, haunches of venison, and delicious smells wafting through the air. Of paradise.

41

It had cooled down overnight, Franza noted with relief. She relaxed by the open terrace door— drinking coffee, enjoying the smell of rain and the fresh breeze coming through the door, and watching the rain form little streams on the tilted windowpanes.

The sound of the water reminded her of the brook from her childhood, which had sometimes overflowed its banks and flooded the house. She felt now as she had then, when they'd had to climb up onto tables. The grown-ups had carried them on their shoulders out of the familiar room, the familiar house. She felt like she was being carried away again, this time out of the familiarity of her life.

Her parents' biggest worry used to be that she'd drown in the brook. They were fanatic about teaching her to swim. Was it happening now anyway? Would they all drown in the whirlpool of events that had swept over them so unexpectedly? Had all those swimming lessons been for naught?

Ben, she thought, *where are you? What have you done?*

Finally she went into his room to look for clues, for evidence. She didn't look for long before she found the scribbled notes on the desk and in the wastepaper basket. With some effort, she managed to decipher them.

Marie in the streetcar,
Marie, the lovely.
Marie, the tiny.
Marie in the streetcar.

. . .

Only Marie has the key to my heart. Mouse rhymes with louse rhymes with Klaus.

. . .

The bit of apple peel stuck between her teeth would always be his way—

. . .

That's all she was able to decipher, but she remembered that Ben's language teachers had always thought he had talent.

42

Half past six. It was still early and time seemed to stand still. Max came in for breakfast, and she was surprised. "You're up already?"

He raised his eyebrows and gave her a baffled look. "It's Friday. I open the office at eight on Fridays, remember?"

She nodded but didn't say anything—nothing about Ben, nothing about what happened the day before. She felt as though Max didn't belong to her anymore; it was none of his business.

"I'm moving out," she said. "I'll look for an apartment in town."

He was surprised, but he nodded and sat down next to her. They looked out to the garden, at the dripping bushes, listened to the wind and the rain.

"Why now?" he asked.

She didn't know how to answer him. Everything was too complicated and mixed up: the dead girl, Ben, Max's child in Sweden, the twins.

"Felix is becoming a father again," she said. "Twins, believe it or not!"

He nodded. "Yes, I know, he told me last night. Why now?"

She wiped her forehead and her eyes. "I don't know. I can't answer that."

"Then the best thing to do is to sell the house," he said softly. "No point staying here on my own."

"No," she said, and turned around briskly. "When Ben comes back . . ."

"Nonsense!" he said. "Ben's not coming back. Ben's living his own life, haven't you noticed? There's a girl, and he wants to go to Berlin with her. Love of his life. He wants us to meet her."

She froze. He'd known this all along?

"Yes," he said. "Didn't expect that, did you? Just because I'm a man doesn't mean I'm oblivious. We go to the sauna together from time to time, and sometimes he tells me things. Your son's a grown-up."

She nodded with the painful realization he was right.

"I'm not saying this to hurt you," he said. She nodded again, stood up, and put her cup in the sink.

"There's enough room for both of us here," Max said. "You don't have to go."

She turned to look at him.

"Is it because of him?" he asked. "Do you even think he'll stay in town? He can get engagements anywhere in Germany, and he's not old enough not to want that."

"How do you . . . ?" she began.

He shrugged. "As I said, just because I'm a man . . ."

He got up and hugged her. For a fleeting moment the feeling of their early days returned.

"This girl," she said. "Ben's girl. Her name is Marie. She's the one who was murdered."

He gaped at her incredulously.

"Think about the moving out thing," he said eventually, softly. "You don't have to go. There's enough room. Ben will need us both."

She left. She'd think about it. Not everything was lost yet.

43

He grabbed a bottle of water, got in the car, and drove out of the parking lot, out of town.

Onto the autobahn toward Berlin, past the exit for Lenting, past the rest area. Then he stopped, as he had every day since.

Everything had gone wrong, so damn wrong. But it wasn't his fault; she was to blame. Why had she even started this . . . thing?

It had been great at first. They'd seen each other in the crazy rhythm she dictated. She inspired him and gave him strength. Suddenly he could see clearly again, everything made sense.

But then she'd become more reserved, distant, and she looked at him in a way he didn't like. He didn't know why or when she'd started to change, it had probably been gradual.

Sometimes he had the uncanny feeling she knew who he was and what role he'd played in the life of her mother and how it had ended. But the thought was absurd; everything had been over and done with a long time ago. She couldn't know. He'd never said anything about it, and he knew her mother wouldn't.

She didn't talk about her family anyway, which suited him just fine. Things had happened—black stains on a white background. After all, they'd received piles of reports from social welfare and psychologists—but he was of the opinion things like that were bet-ter swept under the rug. He never had wanted to read all the gory details.

He got out of the car and walked slowly to the shelter with the benches and the table. A young couple was sitting on one of the benches, English. They were wearing hippieish clothes, probably on their way to the festival in town starting tomorrow. He gave them a nod, and they smiled back and didn't pay any more attention to him.

He sat down with his back to them and leaned against the edge of the table. He unscrewed the top of his water bottle and took a cigarette out of the pack.

So this was the place.

He closed his eyes and leaned forward. The images came flood-ing back. He sobbed and shuddered briefly, and then it passed. It had happened here, the first part at least, the part for which he'd already forgiven himself.

"Are you OK?" The couple turned around, looking at him worriedly.

He lifted his arms reassuringly. "Oh, yes, I'm fine. Thank you." They turned away, and he was by himself again.

It was at the corner of the table where the English girl was sit-ting now, that Marie had sat at first—before either of them knew how it would end. Maybe if she hadn't sat in such a dangerous spot, with the pile of rocks behind her, maybe . . .

No, he thought, and shook his head. There's no point wonder-ing what might have been. What's done is done. She shouldn't have started with this, with this . . .

He had called her that afternoon before it started to rain. He wanted to see her after the party, take her out to a fancy restaurant like she deserved. It was supposed to be her night. But she'd made him beg.

She didn't want anything from him anymore. She was going to take the entrance exams, and she'd pass them. It was over. She was going to Berlin and nothing and no one could stop her. It was over, and he'd have to get used to it.

That's what she'd said, her voice firm and steady.

He was dumbstruck. He had begged, pleaded, cried, called her up a second time, and a third time. He felt everything repeating itself; fear was consuming him. It had made a crybaby out of him; it was as if the past had only been yesterday. He felt how everything repeated itself. He talked as if his life depended on it. Finally she said yes.

Then they'd met after her party, and she'd looked so beautiful. He'd imagined it was for him.

44

Franza put the bear on Felix's desk. She set the scraps of paper with Ben's attempts at poetry next to it.

The surprise in Felix's face quickly changed to understanding, and he held up the bear. "So this is what you found in Marie's room? This is what gave you such a shock?"

She nodded and pointed at the pieces of paper. "Those were in Ben's room."

He nodded. "The big love. So it's Ben."

"Yes," she said. "It's my Ben."

"And you can't get hold of him?"

She straightened her shoulders and closed her eyes for a moment. "That's right. Not since that morning."

He got up, went to the window, and looked out. She knew what he saw, knew the view like the back of her hand: the fork in the road, the house across the way, the window with the torn curtains that were never opened, the small balcony full of bright geraniums, and the woman who regularly plucked out the dead flowers.

"I know you're worried," he said finally, and turned around briskly. "Can you do it?"

"Yes," she said. "Of course."

"You know usually . . ."

She interrupted him. "Yes, I know. But I can't be taken off this case. You understand, don't you?"

"Yes," he said without hesitation. "Of course I understand. But we'll discuss everything in advance—no solo actions."

She nodded.

"All right," he said. "Let's analyze this. You know your son quite well—and so do I. Do you really believe he'd be capable of cold-bloodedly dragging someone out of his car and knowingly letting her stumble to her death? The first injury is one thing. Things like that happen in the heat of the moment, they had a fight, arguing back and forth, and one lashes out. We've seen it a million times. You can fix it if you do the right thing. But what followed—no, that isn't Ben! Ben would have done the right thing. Ben's not a murderer!"

He paused and looked thoughtfully at the door, past Franza.

I love you, she thought, *I love you. Thank you my Felix.*

"On top of that," he continued, "Arthur found a bunch of new cigarette butts in the parking lot yesterday. If I'm not mistaken—if I'm not completely wrong—there'll be some matching the ones from Tuesday."

She looked at him questioningly.

"The man," he said slowly, "who helped you through your panic attack yesterday, I think that's our man. Can you describe him? Did he seem familiar?"

She shook her head with surprise. "No. No, I was . . ."

She fell silent, and he realized she was embarrassed. "That happens to the best of us," he said. "Nothing to be embarrassed about."

She smiled gratefully. "I barely remember anything, can you imagine? It's horrible."

He nodded. She thought about his questions. "No," she continued. "I couldn't really see him, he was standing . . . behind me the whole time, if I remember correctly." She sighed. "But what makes you think he's our man?"

Felix scratched his freshly shaved chin. "Firstly, he acted strangely. Secondly, it's just a hunch. Third, it would exonerate Ben. If it had been him there yesterday, you would have known—even if he'd tried to prevent you from recognizing him."

She nodded thoughtfully.

"Have you thought of getting a DNA analysis?"

"Of course," she said and pulled a small plastic pouch out of her bag. It contained hair she'd taken from Ben's brush that morning.

"Does he even smoke?"

She sighed. "Yes, sometimes. That made me worry even more."

"Well," he said. "Half the population smokes. Or a third, at least."

"True," she said. "Though something actually did seem familiar about the man. Something—but what? A smell, an odor?"

"Really?" Felix asked excitedly. "Go on. Focus."

She tried, but without success.

"It doesn't matter, we'll find out," he said. "And Robert will be watching the rest area from now on. Maybe he'll be back. Maybe we'll get lucky."

45

He wouldn't go back there again. It was too dangerous.

Ever since he'd run into that policewoman with the strange name the rest area had become a dangerous place, a place to be avoided. This annoyed him a little, because it had been his and Marie's last place together and he thought he had a right to be there, but he knew he had to be careful now.

But he was absolutely certain she didn't recognize him. He made sure she couldn't see him, staying behind her the entire time. Her awareness had been so limited that there wasn't any real danger.

He knew what an attack like that felt like, how great the loneliness was—the fear of death—and how you weren't aware of anything going on around you.

Overall, he'd become more relaxed. He was no longer starting out of his dreams bathed in sweat or beating himself up for losing Judith—because a life with her would've changed everything.

He had a good life, after all. What else did he want?

His wife let him have her when he wanted, the kids didn't annoy him too much, he went for a run along the Danube every night until he was dripping with sweat, and his job was under control.

Wasn't that all he needed? What else could anyone want? To be consumed by ambition? What for?

But there had been Judith. And then Marie. And now no one.

This morning he'd noticed his first gray hairs, just two, behind his right ear. He'd pulled them out. Maybe everything would just blow over.

46

"Oh, shit!" Felix said, reaching for his cheek. "I forgot Max, the appointment. Because of all that drama with Lauberts!"

He gingerly examined the location of yesterday's suffering with his tongue, and looked surprised. "Strange, it doesn't hurt anymore. I think I don't need to . . ."

"It's fear," Franza interrupted him. "Fear of the drill. You'll see; your tooth won't let you sleep tonight."

"You think?" Felix was genuinely alarmed.

Franza nodded. "I *know*. But don't worry, Borger will be here soon. Maybe *he* can have a look. He's watched Max a few times, just out of interest, you know? He hasn't for a while now, but you know, a doctor like him can do anything. Do you want me to ask him? As a favor?"

She smiled.

"Don't you dare, you nasty woman!" Felix said and picked up his phone.

Franza pictured Frau Brigitte. She was like part of the furniture sitting at the front desk in Max's office. She had been there since forever, always insisting on being called *Frau Brigitte*. Franza could imagine her indignant look and how hurt she would be by the unreliability of mankind as evidenced by Detective Inspector Herz forgetting his appointment.

Felix switched on the hands-free device so Franza could hear Frau Brigitte's rant. She listened with amusement as Felix stammered for a bit at first but soon resigned himself to listening in silence in the face of Frau Brigitte's thorough reprimand. She'd fit him in specially, just because the doctor had asked her so nicely that morning, and now this! If everyone acted this way—no, really—they'd all be drowning in chaos. But thank God, thank God she was there, Frau Brigitte—it was her vocation to keep things in order and running. When was he coming now, anyway, the Herr Inspector? Was she supposed to just sit and wait for him to tell her—and what was all the exciting news from his job anyway? Did they have the murderer yet—he knew the one she meant—and why didn't he tell her a little bit about the case and this murderer? The Frau Inspector never told her anything, she hardly ever showed her face at the office—please give her regards—and was he going tell her when he'd be coming in? Did he think she had all the time in the world!

Felix breathed a sigh of relief when he was done and had an appointment for late that afternoon. Now he needed a schnapps—though less to numb his tooth than to calm his nerves, which were strained enough already thanks to Lauberts, that asshole.

Franza shrugged. "That's our Frau Brigitte," she said. "Priceless. Lauberts is another story."

Lauberts hadn't turned up at the agreed time to have his statement taken down. Not too late and not too early would have been OK, but not at all—no.

They had called, but Lauberts didn't pick up, so they sent a uniformed colleague, who came back empty-handed. There was no one home. So they had gone there themselves and opened the door with a lock pick pulled from the depths of Felix's desk drawers, where it led a peaceful existence until it was needed for an occasion like this one.

It got them inside, but the apartment was empty. As empty as an apartment can be when no one's there.

Felix had been furious. "Goddamn it! We should've kept him! We should've booked him right away! How stupid can you get?"

Franza had tried to bring him back down to earth. "You know very well that Brückl would never have issued a warrant without any evidence."

"But he didn't have an alibi!"

"So what? That's not nearly enough! Even a rank amateur lawyer would have cut us to pieces."

Felix heaved a sigh of resignation. "So what do we do now?"

"Well, put out an APB," she had said succinctly. "What else?"

He calmed down, breathing deeply. "What did he say? Where's his wife again?"

Franza shrugged. "No idea! Wasn't it . . . Italy?"

"Yes, shit! Italy!" Felix shook his head, furious again. "Huge country!" He sighed. "If this isn't an admission of guilt, I'll eat my hat."

Franza had called and made the necessary arrangements to get a search for Lauberts under way. Once again she thought of the DA and the scene after Bohrmann's shooting.

"Just what Brückl's been waiting for," she said. "He'll eat us alive. Finally the case he's been looking for to make his mark: a beautiful young girl murdered—her face perfect for the front pages and TV—and right during the midsummer lull. And we let the murderer get away. What a blow!" She sighed.

The DA was at the point in life they all were. Not yet old—just not young anymore. It was a fact weighing heavily on someone like him. More than once he'd had the bitter experience of young upstarts—*really* young upstarts—passing him on their way up the career ladder.

He was perfectly aware of how this had happened. The others were already on the other side while he had yet to cross the street. The others were already lined up and waiting for their feed at the great career feeding trough while he was still struggling to get there. He'd never gotten his hands on a really spectacular criminal or political case; those always happened somewhere else—in Berlin or Hamburg or other big cities, but never in this town, which he wished he could crunch between his regularly-serviced-by-Max teeth.

He could feel the iron hand of irrelevancy and lack of recognition. It was a catastrophe for someone like him, who was ambitious and hungry and restless. He was gradually beginning to panic with the fear of abysmal failure—the awareness he'd not made it.

The mountain called *career* was beginning to look too steep, the summit too far off. His longing was turning into fear of the permanent night of old age. He was out of breath and the night was closing in on him.

Franza knew all this straight from his wife's mouth, which amused her, but—understandably—provoked him. But she enjoyed her cups of coffee with his wife, who was the neighbor's daughter from her childhood by the brook. Being carried away from their childhood floods on their fathers' shoulders was bonding, and because Franza didn't use her knowledge to her advantage and because Sonja Brückl needed a shoulder from time to time, Franza lent her one.

Franza always maintained, when discussing the subject with Felix, that if it weren't for her and her shoulder, the Brückls wouldn't even be the Brückls anymore.

"Are you two having coffee again?" Felix asked grimly. He obviously hadn't regained his sense of humor yet. "To discuss the latest blow?"

Yes, that's what it was. A blow. But it couldn't be helped; they just had to keep going. And that's what they did, taking Lauberts's slippers, which they'd found under the bed, back with them for DNA analysis. He'd taken his toothbrush wherever he'd run off to, damn him!

They'd completely screwed this up! They could have easily had his DNA ages ago—he'd drunk water in their office, and there'd been a dirty glass with him all over it. They should have asked him if he wanted to smoke.

But they hadn't! What a screwup! Just because he didn't *look* like a murderer. What the hell did a murderer look like anyway? Only now that he'd disappeared . . .

As soon as they had arrived back at the precinct, they sent a young uniformed colleague to Borger with the shoes and a note attached that read "URGENT!"

Then they had gotten on their phones: one to locate the children's boarding schools, the other the wife's holiday destination. Both proved difficult.

Finally they reached the schools, the elite institutions they'd expected. Lauberts hadn't turned up at either of them, which they'd also expected. Still another blow. He might've wanted to see his kids.

47

Borger arrived and they immediately quizzed him about the slippers. His expression turned strangely indignant, somehow reminding Franza of Frau Brigitte. "I'm good, thanks," Borger said. "How are you?"

"Sorry," Franza said. "But the slippers!"

Borger shook his head uncomprehendingly. "What slippers?"

If Felix hadn't regained his bad mood completely already, he did now. "What do you mean?" he thundered. "What do you mean: what slippers?"

Borger shrugged, took one of the visitors' seats, and loosened his tie. "I have no idea what you're talking about. Could someone perhaps enlighten me?" He smiled in Arthur's direction. "The young colleague, perhaps?"

Franza had to grin despite herself. *Indeed*, she thought. *Is he actually turning gay in his old age?*

She tapped his shoulder and told him Lauberts's story from the beginning. When she was halfway through, someone knocked on the door. The young uniformed police officer stood in the doorway, still holding the plastic bag with the slippers.

"I couldn't find him," he said. "There's only one Dr. Berger in the entire hospital, and he's a psychiatrist and didn't know what to do with the slippers."

"Borger," Borger said and smiled. "Not Berger, dear boy, Borger."

"Oh!" the man said, bracing himself against the doorjamb in order not to fall over.

Shit, Franza thought, *why is everything going wrong today?*

"Well, now you've found me." Borger smiled.

"Yes," muttered the young man, deeply embarrassed. "I have."

Franza looked at Felix and knew he was about to explode.

"Out!" he said, trying hard to hold his breath. "Get out!"

"Yes," the young man whispered. "OK. I'm already gone."

He turned pale, took a step back, and was about to close the door when Felix's voice roared: "STOP!"

The whole room seemed to shake. Arthur thought admiringly: *Wow!* Borger studied his fingernails, and Franza decided to consult an ear specialist sometime soon. The young man froze and feared for his life for a moment.

"The shoes," Felix asked, perfectly calm again. "Do you want to take them with you again? Maybe try Dr. Berger one more time?"

"Yes," the young man whispered, utterly unnerved. "No."

Carefully he placed the plastic bag with the shoes on the floor, stepped out into the corridor, and closed the door so quietly they couldn't hear a sound.

"Jesus," Borger sighed, looking at Arthur. "Young people today."

We could pass for a cabaret, Franza thought resignedly, closing her eyes for a few seconds. *If it weren't so serious, they could turn us into a nightclub act with buffoons and clowns.*

"OK," she said. "Enough. When can we have your results, Borger? As you may have noticed, it's urgent."

"As always," Borger sighed. "I'll get right onto it. But can I first share my news?"

He could. And it was worth it.

"The cigarette butts," he said. "The ones from yesterday. Bingo. One hundred percent match with the DNA from Tuesday."

Franza swallowed, a light shiver running down her spine. Felix's suspicion had been right. *Good old sleuth,* she thought tenderly and was grateful for his hand on her back.

Borger raised his eyebrows. "Have I missed something?"

"Yes," Felix said slowly. "You have indeed. It's getting hot."

He looked out the window with the rain lashing against it and the wind howling, and tapped his finger against the glass. "But don't take it too hard. Here's the short version for you."

When Borger had heard about the murderer's interaction with Franza, his eyes were wide.

"Yes, but the hair you gave me," he said, "that's a mystery. It doesn't match anything. Sorry to disappoint you."

Franza closed her eyes, smiled, and breathed a sigh of relief. A weight was lifted from her—a stone, a huge boulder. At least she didn't have to worry about her son's innocence. "Thank you," she said. "Thank you. When this is over I'm taking you all out to dinner."

Strange day, Borger thought, perplexed, and looked at Felix for help, but he only grinned.

"Are you two OK?" he asked, looking from one to the other. "Are you sure this case isn't getting to you?"

Franza turned serious. "Yes," she said. "I am now. Now I'm sure."

Frowning, Borger sat down on the windowsill. "Am I supposed to get it?" He looked at Arthur. "Do you get it?"

Arthur shook his head. "No, not everything. But I'm used to it." He grinned. Borger sighed.

"That's what I was afraid of. But speaking of dinner . . ." He had the report of what was in Marie's stomach.

"This might actually help you," he said mysteriously, spreading his notes carefully in front of them. "Our girl had a fancy dinner. You don't eat something like this every day, and more importantly, not everywhere."

For sure, Felix thought. He gulped down a cup of coffee while Borger went into a detailed description of all the delicacies Marie Gleichenbach had consumed that night, just so they could be removed from her stomach and analyzed by tie-Borger.

He finished his presentation with effusive praise for the protein content of anything swimming around in the ocean, followed by a lecture directed at Felix about the importance of aforementioned proteins for the health and fitness of certain parts of the body.

"Well," Felix said, grinning. "My loins seem to be doing just fine without me eating that stuff—I'm becoming a father again. Twice over, actually!"

Borger was amazed. "You don't say! Good for you, old stud!"

They decided to celebrate Felix's growing family over a few drinks that evening. *Men, fatherhood, and alcohol,* Franza thought and had to laugh. *What a cliché!*

"Every French restaurant, every Greek and Italian, just every restaurant offering Mediterranean cuisine," Franza instructed Arthur. "And, of course, every seafood place. Maybe we'll be lucky and someone will remember something."

Arthur didn't seem overly enthusiastic. "But I'm working on Frau Hauer."

Felix waved dismissively. "Forget about her. Old news, she's out. That tired unhappy relationship trail has gone cold."

"But," Arthur said, "it makes sense. Marie stole her lover. So she might have . . ."

"No, it wasn't her, believe me. I've got a nose for these things. What do you smell, Franza?"

"The same." She shrugged regretfully at Arthur.

"Well, then, we've all agreed. So, what are you waiting for?" Felix gave Arthur an encouraging look. "Sometimes that's just the way it is: a thousand hours of hard work just to find one piece of the puzzle—you'll have to get used to it if you want to grow old here. And you want to, I can tell by looking at you."

Is that so, Arthur thought, *and what do you see? Boogers? Snot dripping? Bullshit!*

"Cheer up," Franza said looking out at the relentless rain. "I know it'll be a lot of running around, but at least it's a nice day for it."

"That's life," Felix said. "Take Robert with you so you can divide the restaurants between you. Don't forget Marie's photo."

"Well, looks like we made our young colleague's day," Borger said.

"Yes," Franza said. "You could say that."

48

Dinner had been a success. He knew she loved seafood, so he'd reserved a table at the most expensive seafood restaurant in town. The restaurant had two private rooms for its wealthiest customers to dine in undisturbed. He'd booked one of them, which had made the evening a whole lot more expensive, but he couldn't risk being seen with her. Not when things had not yet been decided.

Jumbo shrimp appetizers followed by entrées of sea bass on char, grilled vegetables, and puree of truffles. For dessert, two kinds of chocolate mousse with raspberry sauce. He'd ordered champagne to go with the meal—Moët & Chandon—the most expensive on the menu.

"You can see what you're worth to me," he'd said. She'd been reserved at first, and he'd noticed it right away. She hadn't accepted his present—his wife was wearing the pearls now.

Never mind, he'd thought. She'll come around.

The dinner had been perfect; they wanted for nothing. The table decorated in cream and silver, the white flowers, the polished glasses. Marie in that dress that could have been a wedding dress— the strings of pearls gray and translucent like the rain on that day, and today.

49

Marie's essays showed sensitivity, her handwriting was clean and smooth, her grammar and syntax good. But other than that, one and a half hours of searching her room proved fruitless. No trace of a list of names, no phone numbers.

Franza sighed. It was painstaking, as always. Searching and searching without even knowing what you're searching for. Solving mysteries that ended up not being mysteries at all.

At least they'd found bank statements, showing Marie was not exactly poor. The inheritance from her grandfather had lived on not only in her soul, but also as a considerable amount in her bank account. In addition, her statements showed a steady stream of deposits into her account. There was a generous monthly transaction, probably from her parents, but far more interesting were the large cash deposits made at irregular intervals—apparently the fees paid by certain men for certain services. Arthur would visit the bank later to ask the details.

The apartment was quiet. Everyone had gone to work or to school. The only one there was a young intern who'd retreated to the office to be left in peace.

Then someone knocked at the door of Marie's room, loudly and vehemently. Cosima.

"Hey," she said. "Can he go?" She nodded toward Felix, who immediately lifted his hands in surrender.

"I'm already gone," said Felix. *Wham!* he thought of his first impression of her. *She'll just knock me down if I don't go voluntarily.*

"You're here? I thought . . ." Franza began with surprise.

Cosima shook her head. "Never mind."

She took her time, walking beside the bookshelves, brushing the spines with her index finger. Then she leaned against the windowsill and looked out at the street.

We all do that, Franza thought, *all the time, looking out of windows, at streets, at houses, at the sky, trees, the countryside, the rain. What do we think we'll find?*

"My name's Cosima," Cosima said eventually and turned around. "Did you know that?"

Franza nodded and Cosima continued, unperturbed. "My father's an average-to-bad orchestra conductor. Wagnerian, if you know what that is. He called everyone around him Cosima— his dog, the cat, me, even my mother, although she already had a name. He thought it was . . . uncompromising. What do you think?"

"Strange," Franza said.

"No," Cosima said. "Not strange. Crazy! Stupid! What a bunch of shit! Would you want to be called *Cosima*?"

Franza shrugged. "*Franza*'s not exactly the greatest."

Cosima ignored the comment. "She was an anti-Semite, Cosima Wagner, she was in cahoots with Hitler. Did you know that?"

Franza nodded.

"And yet he named me after her. I can't forgive him for that. But it doesn't matter, there's so much I can't forgive him for."

She looked out the window again, and then after what seemed an eternity said, "Is Pooh still here? Have you found him?"

Franza's heart beat faster. "Pooh?"

Cosima became impatient. "Yes, Pooh! Don't be so slow! It belonged to Ben—you must know that! Or are you just as ignorant as the rest of them?"

"Ben? What do you know about Ben?"

Cosima's gaze was unfathomable. "Jenny's going to kill me," she said with a sigh. "But I guess I'll survive."

She grinned, but then her serious expression returned immediately. "She doesn't trust you. She doesn't trust anyone. I do, though. I know how he used to talk about you."

"Who? About whom?"

Cosima shook her head and looked at Franza with contempt. "You really aren't very bright, are you? Ben, of course! About you—his mother! You're his mother!"

Franza was speechless. What else did this girl know?

"How . . . ?"

"How do I know this?"

She flicked an invisible speck of dust off her sleeve. "He brought photos from time to time. Marie was crazy about photos—family photos, if you know what I mean. Christmas, Easter, birthdays, just happy families. We're all crazy about them."

She gave a mournful laugh. "So Ben brought them along and told us what it was like in a so-called happy family at Christmas and Easter. Then Marie would cry her eyes out, and he'd have to hold her. She was awesome, our Marie. Really a great chick, but sometimes she was just nuts."

She fell silent again and looked out the window, trembling slightly. She shook it off. "Sometimes we got to look at the pictures, too, Jenny and me. He told us lots, Ben. That you're a cop, for example, and that you have a boyfriend, an actor, who's younger than you."

Franza blushed as Cosima's eyes examined her from head to toe, stopping at her hips, which were too wide and too . . .

"But who gives a shit. Your husband cheated on you, too, and probably still is." Cosima raised an eyebrow indifferently and paused for a moment. "We know about the whole family—even the little half sister in Sweden."

Her voice had become mocking and her eyes sharp. Franza felt she was being tested again. Eventually Cosima shook her head. "That's all really ordinary stuff, you know. Don't think Ben's a gossip just giving away all your family secrets." She laughed. "Although I guess that's what he did. But only to cheer us up, to show us that happy families aren't always happy, either. But we already knew that."

Franza felt bad. "So he's unhappy?"

Cosima was surprised. "No," she said, "of course not! Don't you know that?"

"I hoped so. But I . . . I didn't realize he knew everything. That his father and I . . ." She shook her head, the look in Cosima's eyes silencing her.

This wasn't about her and her life, which, apart from a few minor hiccups had gone relatively well so far. No one had beaten her up as a teenager or raped her or threatened her or put her out on the street. Apart from a few floods, she'd grown up peacefully and had had time to prepare for life. So who did she think she was, complaining about her petty problems?

And Ben? What had he been doing here?

Ben, who'd grown up so fast she hadn't even noticed. How withdrawn he'd become. And how he was living his own life, taking responsibility, being in love—deeply and truly it seemed.

And now?

Marie was dead and Ben was God-knows-where.

She felt a stinging pain deep inside her. How could she have thought even for one second that Ben . . .

It had taken this girl to dissipate the last of her doubts.

That's how little she knew him. How little she knew *of* him.

"What's the matter?" Cosima came right up to her and looked her in the face. "You all right?"

Franza nodded. "Where did you meet? Here?"

"Here?" Cosima laughed. "Don't be silly. No, Ben never came here. She would never have brought him here."

"Why not?"

She shrugged. "When you love something, you keep it to yourself. Then no one can take it from you."

What logic, Franza thought and had to smile. *Young girl's logic. Secret logic.*

"But it didn't work," Cosima said quietly. "Nothing ever does."

She cleared her throat. "We met in bars. Or down along the Danube, in the meadows. It's nice there."

Silence again. Franza waited. Marie's secret life. They must be getting close to Marie's secret life. Time was running out.

"Cosima," she said. "You wanted to tell me something."

Cosima looked up, returning from wherever she had been in her thoughts, and shook her head. "No," she said. "No more. Jenny's going to kill me."

She walked to the door, looking small and lost. *I screwed up,* Franza thought, *oh shit, I really screwed up.*

"Cosima," she said, trying to keep her from leaving. "You can trust me! Please, trust me! Tell me what you know."

Cosima stopped. "Ask Ben," she said. "I don't know anything."

"I can't ask Ben," Franza said. "He's gone, and I don't know where he is."

Cosima hesitated for a brief moment, began to waver, but then she shook her head almost imperceptibly.

"Sorry!" she said. "Too bad. I've got to go." She opened the door, and there, sitting on the floor, leaning against the wall, was Jenny.

"Just give it to her," Jenny said. "You're probably right. She'll know what she's doing—she's Ben's mother, after all. So tell her."

Franza held her breath and time seemed to stand still. Finally Cosima turned around, pulled something from the pocket of her jeans, weighed it in her hands for a moment as if thinking it over carefully one more time, and handed it to Franza.

"Here," she said. "We found it in one of her desk drawers. We thought we should check her room after we saw her in the newspaper. We felt we owed her that much. We thought we could . . . we didn't know yet that you . . ."

"What is it?" Franza asked. She felt her heart racing and her breathing becoming faster.

Cosima lifted her eyebrows haughtily. "Well, look at it! Or can't you even read?"

Then she left the apartment with Jenny right behind her.

Franza stared at the little package in her hand. It was wrapped in blue tissue and tied with a piece of string. Then she started running down the stairs toward the front door. Felix was sitting at the bottom of the stairs looking at her expectantly. The girls were walking down the road at a leisurely pace, their hands in their pockets.

"Thanks!" Franza called out waving the package in the air. "Thanks!"

The girls both lifted a hand at the same time without turning around. Then they turned a corner and were gone.

Franza and Felix went back to Marie's room, sat down at her desk, and carefully untied the parcel. It contained a page from a newspaper folded several times—a carefully cut-out article. The paper was old and torn in places. It was almost illegible along the folds. Someone had written a date from more than twenty years ago at the top. The package also contained a photo showing a group of young people sitting around a campfire. Two heads had been circled—those of a young man and a young woman.

They knew immediately this was their breakthrough.

50

Felix's cell phone rang. It was Arthur. He was angry because he wasn't getting anywhere. Neither he nor Robert had found a thing. There were more restaurants that served the cuisine they were looking for than either of them had realized. From the prices, he also was beginning to realize how little money he earned.

"Well," Felix said, unmoved, "I can't help you there. You just need to keep looking. Make sure you check them all today. We're at a critical point, which means longer hours—but you know that."

Arthur hung up with a sigh. Working late yet again. He checked his watch and felt his stomach rumble at the same time. The next restaurant on his list was a seafood restaurant with a French name: Au Bord de la Mer. Very fancy, very expensive—not his cup of tea. And he didn't have an expense account regardless. He headed for the nearest fast-food place.

He wolfed down two hamburgers with fries and a Coke. He could just imagine how his meticulous, muesli-eating mother would throw up her hands in horror at this monstrosity dripping with fat. But weren't mothers there to be emancipated from?

Yielding to an urge, he treated himself to a strawberry shake with extra ice cream and whipped cream and a muffin. Life wasn't so bad after all. In the morning he'd do a couple of extra laps in the park, and everything would be fine.

Full and satisfied, he got back in the car and only swore a little out of habit when he took a wrong turn. For the thousandth time he thought of the hot-blooded Karolina, which dampened his mood again. He finally parked in front of the exclusive restaurant, finding it impossible to imagine Marie eating here. It was the type of posh place where you only went if you had plenty of cash or masochistic inclinations.

Arthur, in any case, had neither. He really didn't feel like spending all night hopping from one eatery to another and was convinced that he wouldn't find anything of use anyway. He got out of the car and sighed.

Shit, he thought, *shit! Another night completely wasted!*

On the other hand, if he was honest, he had nothing better to do. Which he viewed as a medium-sized catastrophe. Karolina had put his hormone production in overdrive without providing the necessary release, which felt disastrous at his relatively young age. He'd heard hormonal congestion could be quite damaging. Furthermore, it didn't look like anything would change anytime soon. Absolutely nothing for three weeks. Not a single woman had cast a benevolent eye on him, not to mention anything beyond that. But was that really surprising? Overworked as he was, he had bags under his eyes and looked slightly insane.

He sighed again and glanced at himself in the rearview mirror. Yes, he realized with a shock, he looked terrible and desperate.

I'll grow old without even noticing it, he thought with frustration, his mood plummeting further. *I'll have had no private life but will solve ten thousand murders. And I won't even have any grandchildren to tell the stories to. At the end of my life I'll be a lone wolf returning to the forests of the north. Better than nothing.*

Nicely expressed, he thought contentedly, *but I shouldn't have eaten so much. I'm going to get a potbelly!* He entered the restaurant and was immediately struck by the decadence of the atmosphere. He stopped at the door, unsure how to proceed. A man in his fifties dressed in a black suit with an elegant tie—the maître d', Arthur assumed—quickly approached him.

"How can I help you?" he asked, running his eyes disapprovingly down Arthur's suede jacket and jeans. His gaze stopped at the tiny squirt of ketchup that was almost completely soaked up by the suede.

"Police, Homicide Division," Arthur said and presented his ID, amused as always at the effect of this statement. "I'd like to ask you some questions."

The distinguished man gave a subdued cough.

"May I ask you to take a seat here for a moment?" he said, and led Arthur to a small table off to the side, in a niche by the window. "This way we won't attract attention. So how can I help?"

Arthur pulled the photo from his jacket pocket. "I'd like to know if this young woman dined here last Monday night between ten at night and one in the morning."

The maître d' gasped with shock when he looked at the photo. "But that's . . . that's . . . the girl from the newspaper."

Arthur nodded.

"And you think she . . . ? Here in our restaurant . . . ?"

Arthur didn't reply.

The maître d' shook his head. "No, I've never seen her before. However . . . Monday was my day off. I'll show the photo to my colleagues if you'll allow me."

He paused for a moment, folded his hands, and put them up to his pursed lips. "Although I really can't imagine her . . ."

He cleared his throat and gestured around the room. "I mean, you can see for yourself, our restaurant is . . ."

"Not suited for the lower classes?" Arthur finished the sentence, causing the maître d' to break out in a fit of coughing.

When he'd recovered, the maître d' made one last attempt. "Why is this so important anyway?"

Arthur sighed. "We're trying to get a picture of her last few hours alive, and any small detail might be of importance. So could you please ask your colleagues? Otherwise I'll have to, and I probably won't be as discreet as you."

The man coughed slightly again, took the photo between his thumb and index finger as if it were poisonous, smiled unhappily, and disappeared.

Poor bastard, Arthur thought.

When he returned he was accompanied by a Marilyn Monroe–like buxom blonde. She was easy on the eyes in her tight skirt and fitted blouse, which showed off her curves.

"My colleague," the maître d' said in a surprised tone of voice, "does indeed have some information for you."

Arthur stood up politely, and the woman smiled into his eyes and nodded as he presented his ID. When she continued to smile, ignoring the ID, he started to feel a little stupid, wondering if her deep smile wasn't directed at him at all. Then they sat down.

51

"I'm going to Berlin," she'd said. "We can't meet anymore. You'll have to find someone else. Or you could try monogamy for a change."

She giggled but quickly turned serious again. "Your wife's lovely—why do you cheat on her?"

"Don't be stupid!" he said. "She's nothing."

They were quiet a moment. "All right," he said then. "Go to Berlin. I'll come with you. I'll leave my wife. We'll get married, and I'll find a new job."

Marie laughed, stabbing at her fish. "You're crazy," she said. "No, you'll do no such thing."

"Yes," he said. "Yes I will. I can't lose you again."

She lifted her head and gave him a strange look. "What do you mean again?"

"Nothing," he said. "Nothing at all."

But she already knew anyway.

52

"Yes I do have information," the Monroe look-alike said. She'd finally released Arthur's eyes, pursed her lips, and was tapping the photo on the table with the perfectly manicured fingernail of her right index finger.

"Of course I recognize her. She was in the private room with her guy. They came in Monday night around ten o'clock, acting like they didn't want to be recognized by anyone." After a brief pause she added, "At least *he* was."

She fluttered her blue eyelids, laughing a deep, cooing laugh.

"Why didn't you contact us earlier?" Arthur asked. "Her picture was all over the newspapers."

She tilted her head to one side and put on a rueful expression. "Oh, you know," she said, "unfortunately, I'm not much of a newspaper reader. I never got into it. But now you're here, thank God."

She beamed at him sincerely, which made his heart beat faster.

"He was so hot for her, I can tell you that," she said with some amusement. "Horny as a bull, excuse the expression. I can tell things like that, believe me."

"I have no doubt about it," Arthur said, losing himself in Monroe's eyes, which were at least as blue as her eyelids. He realized he was feeling the same way about her. "Yes," he said. "I bet you can tell with absolute certainty. But can you describe the man, too?"

She could.

She described him so thoroughly and accurately that Arthur's jaw dropped. He imagined Marilyn must have spent two hours standing next to the poor man, devouring him with her eyes.

"Wow!" Arthur said admiringly. "I'm blown away! Would you mind coming by my office tomorrow so we can prepare a sketch? We hardly ever get such a detailed description. You're incredibly observant."

She gave him a pleased smile, and he was sure she had talents in other areas as well. Then she surprised him again.

"Yes," she said, slowly licking her bottom lip. "I am, aren't I, Herr Detective? But I have to admit I had plenty of time to study him closely. After all, I spent two years in his class."

53

At dinner, she asked, "Do you know where I'm from?"
And he said yes, he did. He'd known from the start.

. . .

The name had made him sit up at first. He used to know a carpenter named Gleichenbach in his village. Then the principal's secretary brought her into his classroom, and she stood there. He looked at her, and he stopped breathing. The room began to sway, and his legs practically gave way.

He asked the secretary to take over for a moment—just for a short while. They were writing an exam . . . all she had to do . . . he really needed to, just quickly . . .

He walked out of the room, ignoring the puzzled look on the secretary's face and the students' giggling. Then he started to run, which calmed him down. When he reached the staff toilet he locked himself into a cubicle, leaned against the wall, tried to stop shaking—to breathe—and inhaled two cigarettes so deeply his lungs burned.

Had he seen a ghost?

He soon found out that it was much simpler than that. She was the daughter of the carpenter from his village. But more importantly, she was Judith's daughter.

"Everything all right?" the secretary asked with a sneer when he returned to his classroom. "Did you see a ghost?"

He smiled uneasily. "No, no, don't worry, I just remembered . . ."

She shook her head and left.

The class had been taking a chemistry exam. Judith's daughter looked at him with Judith's eyes out of Judith's face.

He cleared his throat. "Your name?" he asked.

"Gleichenbach," she said. "Marie." And smiled.

She hit on him. She could sense that he wanted her. She could always sense things like that.

He was slightly annoyed. Until now he'd never had to pay for sex. But she was Judith's daughter. That changed everything.

She called him at the most impossible times from the most impossible places and ordered him to come. "That's just how I do things," she had said with a little smile. "That's how I do it with all of them."

She didn't even pretend he was the only one. In a soft voice she told him what and how she'd already done it with the others, and what she'd do in the future, while his breathing became hoarse and he drowned in her.

He lost control as she chased him from climax to climax, like a tiger chasing its prey. Often he lost all sense of time and Marie and Judith became one and the same.

If anyone had told him he was plunging headfirst into disaster, he wouldn't have believed it.

• • •

They drank champagne. It tickled as it went down. She barely touched her fish.

"Listen," she said. "I've fallen in love."

"With me?" he asked. "That's good."

"No," she said. "No, not with you. You know that."

He gave her a dark look. We can solve this problem, *he thought.*

She brushed her hand through his dark hair. "You're smart and handsome," *she said. His heart twitched, it sounded like good-bye.*

We can solve this problem, *he thought again.*

Before dessert he slid his hand between her legs. He traced her collarbone with his tongue, and then her neck. "You taste so good," *he whispered.*

She hesitated at first, but then she let him continue. "No charge today," *she said.* "Because it's the last time, and because I'm happy."

He nodded, feeling humiliated, but he nodded. They drank champagne; it tickled in their throats.

· · ·

She ran out into the rain, arms wide open, and said: "Take me to Berlin."

"When?" *he asked.* "Now?"

"Yes!" *she shouted into the rain.* "Now, right now, and we'll be there by the morning!"

"Yes, OK, I'll take you to Berlin. I'd drive you anywhere, wherever you want to go."

He took this for a good sign. It fueled his hopes. He was tipsy enough—they hadn't stopped at one bottle.

· · ·

They had stopped at the rest area because he needed to pee. When he returned, she was sitting on a bench underneath the ugly tent-like shelter, talking on the phone. That was when he first began to see red. He sat down next to her, but she just kept talking as if he wasn't even there. That irritated him.

"Great," she said. "So we'll meet there tomorrow. You'll have to get up early. Yes, one o'clock. I'll be there."

She laughed. Cooed. "I can't wait to see you."

Like a pigeon, *he thought,* disgusting.

Then he confronted her. "What's that supposed to mean, 'one o'clock; I'll be there.' What's all that about?" he asked. "Who did you call? Who are you meeting tomorrow?"

She gave him a blank look. "That's none of your business," she said.

Her bluntness had pushed him over the edge. "What are you trying to say?" he shouted. "I'm driving you to Berlin, remember? So I think it's damn well my business if you're meeting someone else there!"

She glared at him. "You already got your reward tonight, remember?"

He thought he was dreaming. How could he have been so wrong?

"But I love you," he said. "We're going to Berlin together."

She shook her head, stunned. "No," she said. "No, we aren't."

"I'll leave my wife," he said. "I told you! Only an hour ago! And I'm coming to Berlin with you."

"No!" she said. "No!"

She shrank back slightly, as if she sensed danger, like a faint vibration in the air.

He laughed, trying to defuse the situation.

"Come on," he said. "Relax. Don't be so serious. Where's your smile? I've got a bottle of wine in the car. I'll get it and we'll crack it open. Then you can tell me all about this guy you've been talking to. And then we'll tell him to forget about it, OK?"

He stood up and walked to the car, getting the bottle and a corkscrew from the trunk. "I'm afraid we'll have to drink from the bottle," he said. "I don't have any glasses for madame."

He bowed gallantly and waited for amused laughter. But it didn't come. She was in defense mode.

"Listen," she said. "There's something you don't understand, and I want to sort it out once and for all. I'm going to Berlin with Ben. Not with you, but with Ben. Ben's a friend—my boyfriend. We're both going to school there, and we're going to live together. I'm meeting him tomorrow at one o'clock at the train station. Do you understand?"

He just stood there, bent forward, breathing heavily. He was holding the bottle in one hand and the corkscrew in the other. His eyes had narrowed to hostile slits. His mouth had taken on a bitter expression.

Marie's heart contracted with fear. She lifted her arms.

"Don't worry about taking me to Berlin," she said, frightened by the trembling in her voice. "It's just too far, and we're both tired. Let's just go home now. I'll take the train in the morning."

Slowly she edged closer to him. She wanted to touch his face and comfort him in her good-bye.

He slapped her hand away, angry, hurt. The bottle slid out of his hand and went flying through the air, crashing onto the pavement and narrowly missing the car. The bottle broke with a muffled sound and the wine disappeared in the rain. He took out a cigarette, and then another.

. . .

With some effort, they both calmed down.

Because they knew there was no other way. Because they knew they had to calm down. They had to do something, soon. They couldn't stay here forever, at this stupid rest area under this stupid roof.

He went and got another bottle from the car.

Cautiously, Marie suggested that maybe that wasn't such a good idea. Maybe they'd had enough to drink, and they still had to get back to town. If they got caught at a police checkpoint, he'd lose his license.

He gave her a dark look and tried to think of what to do. Then he sent the second bottle flying and started to laugh. He laughed and laughed until he wasn't sure if he'd ever be able to stop, until he wasn't sure if he was still laughing or if he was crying.

Finally, after what seemed like an eternity, Marie sat down next to him. He began hoping again, and told her he longed for her, he longed for her so much.

He asked her to sleep with him one more time, here and now. He started to beg, brushing her neck with the back of his index finger. He felt her tremble. "Come on, please!" he said and felt his heart beating faster. He felt alive, like he always did when he was with her. "Baby, do it for me, sleep with me. I need this now, please."

He'd never had to beg before in his life. Women had always been eager to fall into his arms and then into his bed. At first he'd been surprised, but then he got used to it and simply accepted everything they were willing to do for him and give him. They were drawn to his mysterious silence and his eyes, distant and unreadable. It made them want to explore. They didn't understand that he couldn't lose himself. They didn't understand anything, but that didn't matter.

Karen? She was the least important. The least essential. She'd given him an alibi for his search—she was nice, servile, never asked questions. She was a little mouse keeping him warm when he was cold, because sometimes he was cold.

He was always gentle and tender, always gave them what they wanted. But they didn't make him feel alive, none of them, and when he left—and he always left abruptly—they whined and cried and claimed he treated women badly.

He couldn't understand why. He'd never raised a hand against a woman since the one time, so how could they say he treated women badly?

Because he didn't see them and left them alone. Because he drove them crazy but didn't let them get close, protecting himself so they couldn't get under his skin.

But wasn't that what had attracted them in the first place?

That shut them up. And him?

Once—only once—had he experienced the humiliation of being left, the pain of rejection. Back on that terrible afternoon when Judith had walked away and disappeared around the corner in her white tunic and white pants and pinned-up hair, taking his life with her.

Ever since then he had searched. For her, for Judith, for his life. Yet he knew it was hopeless, she was lost to him—forever. Because of that one desperate moment, she was gone forever. As far removed from him as if she'd died.

And then . . . she turned up, this one here. Marie. And brought back the magic feelings lost so long ago.

And now?

She humiliated him. No—worse than that—she was going to leave him. Just like her mother did.

"Come on!" he said. "Come on, let's do it. I need to feel you, right now."

But she said no. No, at least not until they were back in town. Then she'd take him back to her room, sneak him into the building, into her room. It'd be so exciting, an adrenaline rush with Hauer in the office just down the hall. He'd love it, he'd see.

She humiliated him. It pierced through him like a stinger.

She pulled out all the stops to convince him. She wanted to go back. She was getting cold in her light dress. She started shivering, goose bumps on her arms, her nipples hard against her dress. Why did he have to keep looking at her, fondling her?

She pushed him away, gently but firmly.

"Come on," she said. "Let's go. It's cold; I'm freezing. Let's do it later, in my room. I want you."

Her voice was flattering, cooing, but that was a mistake, he saw through it.

Like a pigeon, *he thought,* Disgusting, go fuck yourself you stupid bitch!

"Give it to me!" he said. "Give it to me right now!" He stood with his legs apart, opened his trousers. Nothing was decided yet. Things could still go either way.

But what did she do?

Nothing. Looked for something to talk about and chose the wrong topic. Her mistake.

54

The newspaper article was about a hit-and-run accident in which a nine-year-old girl had died. In the paper her face looked happy and curious, just like a typical nine-year-old.

The detectives ordered the file.

The case dated back more than twenty years and had never been solved. The officer working on the case had retired shortly after, and a year later died of a brain hemorrhage, so they couldn't interview him. There hadn't been a single real suspect back then; no one had seen or heard anything. The storm around the time of the accident would have allowed the person or persons to flee the scene.

The girl and her family had been vacationing from up north, visiting relatives down here. She had been playing by the Danube while her parents had gone to buy groceries for dinner. Pasta was on the menu. Lisa had become friends with the children from the village and wanted to stay while they went shopping. When the storm hit, the other children had scattered.

The parents became worried because of the storm and came back to the beach to look for her. Around the same time, an anonymous woman called the emergency number to notify the police of an accident. She described the scene and asked for an ambulance. But help came too late, and the parents had to take a dead girl home.

"What a tragic story," Franza said, and put the Lisa Fürst file down.

She looked at the photo again. What was its connection to the newspaper article? And what was the connection between the Fürst and Gleichenbach cases?

Franza sighed and held the picture right up to her eyes, but it didn't help. The faces were too small and it was almost impossible to make out anything.

"Maybe this will help," Felix said, handing her a magnifying glass. A few moments later she made a surprised sound.

"What is it?" Felix asked excitedly. She handed him the photo and the magnifying glass. "See for yourself."

It was obvious. Judith Gleichenbach, Marie's mother.

And the man? Long dark hair, headband, athletic, tanned.

Could it be Lauberts? The man they had been trying so hard to find? They weren't sure; they couldn't make him out.

"Never mind," Franza said, leaning back in her chair. "The picture is twenty years old—twenty years changes people."

Felix nodded as he got to his feet and picked up his jacket. "But why puzzle over it if she can just tell us?"

Franza tapped the newspaper clipping with her finger. "And hopefully she can explain the connection."

55

He zipped up his pants slowly, staring at her in disbelief for a few heartbeats. Then horror overcame him.

A name. Lisa Fürst. Did he know it?

Did he? How could she even ask? Where on earth was this coming from?

It was etched into his memory forever, eating away at him like hydrochloric acid in his gut, slowly killing him for more than twenty years now. How could she know?

"Oh my God!" she said, realization gradually dawning on her. He saw it.

She got to her feet as if in slow motion.

"You were driving," she said, stunned. "It was you!"

She swayed a little. The alcohol had loosened her tongue and caused her to stagger now—out of her life and into death. But she didn't know this yet. Neither of them did.

She turned around.

She wants to go, he thought, but it's too late now. It's really too late for that.

She tried to slip past him. "I don't know anything," she said. "Honestly, I don't know anything."

He shook his head. "No," he said, "you really don't know any-thing. I wrestled with myself. I wrestle with myself every single day. You have no idea."

"She was only nine," she said. "Damn it, a nine-year-old girl and you took off."

Her voice became firmer. Her wondering—her astonishment—was waning.

"You killed her!" she shouted. "A little girl!"

She crouched, cowering. "It's always the same! You kill them and then you leave them and you don't care. And then we die again and again while you walk away, back to your lives. And us? We stay right where you left us! Right where you dumped us! And no one sees us ever again, no one."

She whimpered, lost in alcohol and memories.

Good, he thought, she won't cause any trouble.

"Listen. Now listen carefully. I'm taking you to Berlin and we'll forget this ever happened," he said.

"Listen," he said again, his voice hoarse. "Listen, I'm letting you go—just like you wanted."

He raised his arms and walked slowly toward her, wanting to touch her hair, her neck, her face.

"But just one last time," he said in his new hoarse voice and couldn't help himself, couldn't stop himself, "I want to be close to you one last time."

When he touched her, she hissed like a cat. She jumped up, but he'd already grabbed her and was holding her by the throat.

She was too surprised to put up a fight. She gasped and groaned. He heard her choking as if through wads of cotton. And then he let go, pushing her away from him, and she spun around and fell. Just tipped over, all of a sudden. Then . . . the sound as her head hit the rocks, her eyes as she fell, her neck, still pulsing with life.

He ripped open the pack of cigarettes with trembling fingers, struggled to light a cigarette, and smoked it while trying to figure out what to do next. He couldn't think of anything, and so he lit another one.

From the very start, her neck had seduced him. It was the only innocent part of her, the only pure part. It was the part, he imagined, no one else had possessed, only him. And it was still pulsing with life.

He looked down at her, brushing her with the back of his hand, feeling the urge to caress her in her innocence and purity. He felt like he was drowning and closed his eyes wearily, slipping briefly into a world of dreams. She was sitting on top of him, smiling. But then he heard again and again how her head hit the rocks, and how the blood trickled out, forming rivulets and puddles before disappearing among the rocks.

Then he saw the body of the child flying across the windshield and another sound, heavy raindrops hitting his car. The child, her eyes a dull gray—suddenly it all faded away.

Confused, he staggered backward and looked at his hand, covered with blood. Shit, he thought, you bitch! You're ruining everything, you bitch!

"Shit!" he shouted out loud and spun around, once, twice, looking all around, but no one was there. It was three o'clock in the morning.

56

Arthur leaned forward, whistling softly through his teeth. "Tell me everything," he said.

"Sure," Marilyn replied. "Would you like a drink? Champagne, maybe? Or a vodka, on the house?"

"No," he said regretfully, "thank you. I'm on duty."

She took a strand of his hair, which had fallen over his right eye, and brushed it back behind his ear. "What a pity," she said.

He grabbed her hand and smiled. "You're gorgeous, aren't you!" he said, feeling flattered, almost moved.

"Am I?" she said.

A man came to the table. It was the manager of the restaurant, judging by his resolute demeanor. "May I ask what . . ." he began. "Frau Wallner . . ."

Arthur pulled out his ID again. "Police, Homicide Division," he said coolly, "I'm interviewing a witness. You're obstructing a murder investigation."

The man froze for a moment, and then recovered and opened his mouth to ask a question, but Arthur beat him to it. "Ask your headwaiter, he knows. And now I'd be grateful if you'd let me continue my work in peace. Thank you very much."

"All right," the manager said confused. "But if I may ask you to . . ."

"You may," Arthur said, surprised at himself. "Of course you may."

He gave a friendly nod to the man, who raised his eyebrows and walked away.

Marilyn giggled with delight. "Wow!" she said. "You let him have it!"

"Did I?" Arthur said, and felt flattered again. "Now, where were we?"

"My name's Sabine," Marilyn said.

Later, after she'd told him everything and shown him the private room and he'd enjoyed a tiny vodka after all, he thought with a certain degree of compassion that teachers really were poor bastards. They couldn't get away with anything, really couldn't make a single false move. They would always be recognized by someone, and there would always be someone with a score to settle— and who would do so with a smile.

He'd failed her. Without remorse, she said, without an ounce of compassion. He'd raised his left eyebrow a tiny bit and cold-bloodedly failed her.

It happened six years ago. She'd chosen chemistry in her final exams because she thought she could manipulate him with her female charms. Apparently that pissed him off. When he walked past her table during the prep period for the oral exam, she handed him her exam sheet. On it she'd written one single meaningful sentence in pencil.

I'd like to show my gratitude with enthusiasm and persistence.

A smile and a glimpse of her strategically placed, half-opened thighs should have done the rest, but they didn't. He carefully looked over everything she had presented so cleverly, and then looked into her face. She noticed, in addition to his surprise, an amused glint in his eyes. He raised one eyebrow and that had been that.

"Even though," she said, "rumor had it he was after anyone in a skirt. But just not me, unfortunately."

"Well," Arthur sighed.

"Well," Marilyn sighed. "And so I'm stuck here, wasting my time, 'cause every good-looking guy coming through the door already has a date."

Her eyes traveled up Arthur's legs and to his face. She smiled, and he was afraid he'd turned red.

"Except for you," she said and beamed. He beamed too, like a tomato on its way to the ketchup bottle.

Later on she added that the asshole didn't even recognize her when she served him and that little slut their champagne and shrimp and sea bass—though it had only been six years ago. But he'd only had eyes for his little whore. She was sure things had gotten pretty hot in that private room between the main course and dessert, she told Arthur with bright eyes. She'd bet on it, if he knew what she meant.

Yes, he knew. She was hinting so unambiguously he couldn't help knowing.

He learned everything: name, age, likes, dislikes, clothing size, everything.

And as the vodka spread through his body, warming him, he would have liked to warm himself somewhere else, too. If only there'd been time—but there wasn't. Damn Herz! Damn all this overtime!

A short time later he followed her to the door. What a fantastic ass, he thought, overwhelmed.

And he left feeling elated.

57

Judith didn't say anything but they could see she was surprised. She stepped aside, letting the detectives in, and then led them to the living room. They saw immediately that she was packing to leave: empty shelves, boxes stacked high, organized chaos. "I'm moving," she explained. "I'm renting an apartment in town. We're selling the house."

She cleared the table, pulled up three chairs, and turned off the TV, which was showing the evening news. She asked the detectives to take a seat. "I should have done it a long time ago," she said, staring into space. "I'm looking forward to being on my own."

Would they have stayed together, Franza wondered, *my son and her daughter? Would we have met, would we have liked each other?*

"Can I offer you a drink?" Judith Gleichenbach asked, wiping off the table with her hand.

Franza shook her head, as did Felix. "No," she said. "Thank you. How are you doing?"

Judith nodded and shrugged her shoulders. "I'm doing OK. I just have to. I'm going to look for a job."

She paused for a moment, searching for words. Franza spoke first.

"We'd like to show you something," she said. "We found this in Marie's room."

She placed the newspaper article and the photo side by side on the table. Judith leaned forward to look at them, and a moment later she froze. Then she jumped up and started digging in her boxes, throwing books, folders, and other odds and ends onto the floor. Finally she found what she was looking for: a photo album. She opened it with trembling fingers and turned page after page until she was about halfway through. Then she lowered the album and it slipped out of her hands onto the floor, where it stayed.

Judith covered her deathly pale face with her hands. "She took it," she whispered. "She really took it."

Franza got up and leaned down to look at the photo album. She saw there was a picture missing on the opened page. "What?"

"That there." The woman's voice was flat and her eyes glassy. "What you just put on the table."

"Could you please explain?" Franza said and suddenly felt it was urgent. Time was running out because of something they didn't yet know about.

Judith thought for a moment. "About half a year ago she turned up here, just before Christmas. I was . . . surprised. And very happy. She was different—she said she'd met someone. We drank tea and ate gingerbread cookies. She told me her boyfriend's mother had made them. I found it a little strange, but also touching. She was so proud of this . . . normalcy."

She laughed softly, tears streaming down her face.

"Then all of a sudden she wanted to look at photos from when she was little. I gave her two or three albums, but she must've looked at the rest as well."

"Weren't you with her?"

"Not the whole time. I was making her bed. She wanted to stay the night. But when I came back . . ."

She got up, wiping her face. "The albums had been put away. She'd taken the dishes to the kitchen and said she couldn't stay after all; she had to go back to town. There was a bus in ten minutes."

"Did she say why?"

"No." Judith shook her head. "She didn't say, and I didn't ask."

"Why not?"

"Because I knew I wouldn't get an answer. That's just how she was."

"Had she changed?"

Judith shrugged.

"And you didn't ask why?"

Trembling, Judith turned to the window. She was about to lose control.

"Good Lord, if you'd known my daughter you wouldn't be asking questions like that. She either talked when she wanted to or not at all. And most of the time she didn't."

Franza nodded, trying to calm her down. "All right, let's move on. What happened next?"

A deep sigh. "Nothing. She left."

"So she found the newspaper article and the photo. In this album?"

Judith nodded. "Yes, that's what must have happened."

"What's the connection?"

"There is none!"

"And we're supposed to believe that?"

Judith trembled harder and shrugged. "The only connection is that I kept the article on this page of the album."

"Why did you keep the article?"

"I can't remember. It was twenty years ago."

"Did you know the child in the accident?"

"No."

"No?!"

Judith Gleichenbach opened the door to the terrace, letting in a gust of fresh air. She inhaled deeply.

"Frau Gleichenbach." Franza walked over to her and touched her on the shoulder. "Frau Gleichenbach, please help us. It's about your daughter!"

She nodded. "Yes," she whispered. "Yes, I know. About my daughter."

"So, the girl," Felix began. "Her name was Lisa Fürst, and she was here on vacation with her parents. Someone ran over her with a car and then just left her there to die. Whoever was driving just took off—that's called hit and run. That's a serious crime. I think you're aware of that!" Felix held up the article for her to see, his voice had become sharp, angry. He knew that time was running out, too. "Look at her! You knew her!"

Judith shook her head with despair. "No, I didn't know her, and I don't know what you want from me!"

"Oh, just cut it out!" Felix was angry. "Are you seriously trying to tell us you just kept the article for fun? You must have had a reason! And you haven't forgotten it!"

He waited, watching her struggling with herself. *Come on,* he thought, *don't take forever.* He felt tiredness weighing him down the way it always did when difficult cases hit the homestretch but played hard to get right at the end.

Felix looked at Franza and saw she felt the same. They felt like puppets before the impending storm. When it broke, it would crush them. They always sensed that in advance. It was like a tingling in their bones, a turmoil in their guts. Felix knew he shouldn't eat heavy food on those days, but he always did anyway and paid for it by spending hours on the toilet when it was all over, draining himself body and soul.

But that's how it was, plain and simple. It made them old—damned old. They'd be doddering old fools before their time because all these cases sucked the bright, blooming life right out of them. In moments like this he could feel the aging, feel the weariness seeping its way inside him. It felt like he was being torn apart and the youth drained from his body.

He assumed it was the same for Franza. Her face and her eyes said it clearly enough, but he didn't dare ask.

He could also see it when he looked at Borger. His ties seemed to be closing in menacingly around him, while propping up his bulging neck and making his cheeks look chubbier than they actually were.

Maybe Franza was right to allow herself this young actor; maybe it let her feel something long lost. But how long would he be there for her? At some point he'd get an offer from somewhere up north, or from Switzerland—one he couldn't resist. And then what?

Felix saw how Franza swallowed, how her eyelids twitched. She was tired. She'd had too little sleep the last few days. Her body and soul were drained from worrying about Ben and everything else.

"Frau Gleichenbach," she said, "let's not drag this out unnecessarily. We're all tired. Let's bring this to an end. What happened with the girl back then?"

Felix looked at Judith and knew Franza had found the right words. Judith gave in, melted.

"Just once," she said. "I saw her just once."

Felix took a deep breath. "When?"

She remained silent, wiping her face again. Tears continued running down her cheeks. She had time; she'd already lost everything.

"When? Where?"

She shook her head. *Different question,* Felix thought, *change the topic, quick!*

Franza beat him to it. She picked up the photo from the table and pointed to the girl. "Is that you?"

Judith nodded.

"Did you draw circles around the heads?"

"No."

"So Marie did. Why? What's the connection?"

"I don't know." Her desperation—her helplessness—was tangible. She really didn't know, not yet.

"Have you heard the name Lauberts before? Anton Lauberts?"

She thought about it, and then shook her head, repeating the name. "Lauberts? No."

Too bad, Franza thought, *that's a shame.* She tried again. "So the man standing next to you in the picture is not Anton Lauberts?"

She shook her head again, uncomprehending. "No, what makes you think that?"

"Who is it then?"

She looked up. A suspicion crept into her eyes. She shook her head almost imperceptibly, as if wanting to shake off the realization gradually coming over her.

"No," she said and gasped in astonishment. "No. It was twenty years ago. It can't have anything to do with Marie. Please tell me it's got nothing to do with Marie."

"His name," Felix said. "Tell us his name!"

"Johannes," she said.

"Last name?"

She held her breath, her eyes started to flicker. They all held their breath.

"Last name?" Felix asked.

"Reuter," she said. "Johannes Reuter."

They looked at each other. They knew at once they'd heard the name before. Something clicked in their brains, slowly, but it clicked.

Johannes Reuter.

They knew the name, but from where?

It clicked louder, the fog lifted slowly, disappearing like bubbles in a foam bath. Johannes Reuter.

Franza looked at the photo, imagined him without the long hair, added twenty years. Some people were like good wine, only coming into full bloom after many years.

It came clear to them both at the same time. They looked at each other and knew. A full head of hair, athletic build, likeable, good-looking—murderers didn't walk around with signs hung around their necks. Johannes Reuter. English and chemistry. Marie's teacher.

Marie's mother knew it, too.

"How did she know him?" she whispered. "How is all this connected? What happened?"

"Tell us," Franza said. "Tell us what happened back then."

"We were in the car," Judith said in a monotone. "He was driving. Suddenly the girl was there. It was raining, we could barely see. It was a thunderstorm. We'd had a wonderful day, we were planning our future, we were together and in love. But all of a sudden this girl was there, lying on the road. And the rain was beating down on her."

58

She woke up. It startled him; he hadn't expected it. She tried to get up, swayed, and fell back down. "What?" *she said.*

All right, *he thought, feeling some relief,* it's OK. This is going to be all right. Back to town, to the hospital, explain, talk, explain some more, the doctors, the police, his wife, Judith.

He spread a blanket over the backseat of his car and lifted her up. She groaned. He put her on the blanket and carefully placed her head onto a second blanket so that the blood wouldn't ruin his seats.

She won't say anything, *he thought, shaking his head with determination.* I'll save her, and she won't say anything. We'll go to Berlin. Lisa Fürst is all over.

Is it ever all over for death?

He turned on his directional signal as he left the parking lot, his headlights cutting through the darkness. Soon there would be traffic.

She was restless, groaned, tried to sit up. "Stay down," *he said.* "You're hurt. I'm taking you to a hospital."

"No," *she said.* "Don't. Take me home. Take me to Ben." *That had been it. Nothing else.*

. . .

We won't then.

We just won't. But how could she wreck everything?

For the second time. Wreck the dream of love that he'd had for so long.

. . .

Judith had jumped out of the car and left him. He felt it as if it had just happened yesterday. The moment had lasted an eternity. They had been swimming in the Danube, then the thunderstorm, then rushing to the car. They were still laughing, still happy. Then the child in the middle of the road, then the child on the windshield, then the blood and the drumming of the rain.

Both of them had jumped out of the car and run to the child, but she was lying there without moving. There was nothing they could do. A distant melody in the clouds.

He'd spun around, once, twice. There was no one to be seen, just Judith and him. "Get in," he'd said. "We're going."

She turned to him, slowly, staring at him in horror. He grabbed her by the arm and pushed her toward the car. "We're going," he said. "We're going!"

She recovered from her shock and began fighting him. "Are you crazy?" she said. "We can't just . . ."

And she turned around and started walking toward the child, but he grabbed her again, dragged her into the car. She screamed and fought back, and then he hit her.

He screamed into her ear that the child was dead. There was nothing they could do, nothing.

He screamed that his life would be destroyed if they stayed. Is that what she wanted, his life . . . destroyed.

He realized he was still hitting her, again and again, but she . . .

His voice broke, his hand stopped.

. . . she was silent, finally.

He turned around. The rain was washing the blood off the child's head, a girl. This child—this girl—was responsible for this shit! He got into the car and drove away. Judith in the backseat was still shutting the fuck up!

· · ·

He drove and drove. He wasn't sure where to go, but somewhere where he'd be seen, where he'd be remembered. Someplace where they'd say: Yes, he was there! He was definitely there.

In case the cops went looking for him and he needed it later. He heard a sound like a woman's voice in his ears, soft, high-pitched. Judith in the rearview mirror was lying there stiff, stupid bitch, stiff face and stiff eyes. They were all stupid bitches! Then he knew . . . no more love, no more of Judith's love, never again, not on the Danube, nowhere, never again.

The silence and the trembling and the terrible loneliness came afterward. "Get away from me," she'd said. "Never come near me again." Her voice was firm and steady, almost businesslike.

He pulled up outside a pub in town, and she got out. She was swaying a little, and he tried to catch her, to hold her, but she raised her arms defensively. "Don't touch me!" she'd said. "Don't touch me." Then she'd walked away, across the street and into an alleyway he was unfamiliar with. She was limping slightly, and he asked himself why. He hadn't hit her hard enough to make her limp. He couldn't have; it was nothing!

He shook his head and tried to laugh. He succeeded a little. Then he tried to imprint forever on his memory how she looked. It was the last look he would have of her, and it remained his picture of her for all those years. He could see how she disappeared into the alleyway in her bright, almost transparent white dress, low-cut in the front and back with half sleeves; the red straps of her bikini at her neck; her wide linen pants; the purple espadrilles; and her dark hair pinned up hastily. Loose strands of hair hung down, her neck and arms were tanned, and still the rain pouring down. It made her look more transparent than she really was.

He felt a sob inside him, an urge to cry out loud. He wanted to run after her, but already there was an invisible barrier between them. It got larger and larger the farther she walked away from him, and he realized he would never be able to cry on her shoulder again.

Eventually he went into the bar and got drunk. Death tasted of apple liqueur, love of elderberry schnapps, despair of nothing.

All those years no one had ever asked him for an alibi.

No one had ever even mentioned her name to him: Lisa Fürst. And now her of all people—Judith's daughter. Was this Judith's belated revenge, a revenge that she'd never even know about?

. . .

What's life worth? *he thought and felt despair grip him. He hit the brakes and heard Judith's daughter scream as she slid into the gap between the seats. The skinny little girl, skinny enough to fit into the gap—she could stay there.*

Shit, *he thought,* she's making a mess of my car. They always make a mess of my car, from the outside or the inside—why do I always have to deal with this bullshit?!

The road was wet, the car careened to the side, across the shoulder, and into the grass.

Marie groaned between the seats. She'd forfeited all rights, still crying for Ben! Stupid bitches! All of them, stupid bitches!

He'd wanted to change his life, leave his wife and children, make a whole new start—and she?

What did she do? Cried for Ben!

He got out of the car and opened the door behind his seat.

She looked up at him painfully. "My leg," she said, "I think I twisted it."

He didn't reply.

"What are you doing?" she asked, astonished as he grabbed her under the arms. She screamed out in pain. Then he let go.

"You're doing it again," she said with a trembling voice. He could sense she was afraid. It gave him a strangely exhilarated feeling. He the cat, she the mouse—death between them.

She passed out again, all of a sudden. Shock, maybe?

He just stood there, wiping his face with his hand. He felt it was wet, but didn't know whether it was from the rain or because he was crying. They were the same tears as twenty years ago. They felt the same as they had then, so painful, so raw. She wanted to leave him again. Wanted to walk into the alleyway in her bright white clothes, the color of summer on her arms and neck, translucent in the rain.

. . .

"You're doing it again," she'd said. "You're doing it again!"

No! Not him! She was doing it!

He could hardly believe what was happening. History was repeating itself. The rain, the road, the blood, the girl.

"No!" he said. "No, it's not like that. NOT like that!"

He looked away with a rigid gaze, wiping his face again and again, realized now that this wetness came from him, from his heart, because she was dying now, the one he'd loved. She'd weigh on him like lead from now on, inseparable. Wasn't that what he'd wanted?

When he dragged her out of the car, she groaned, holding her head, and woke up.

"No," she said. "No, don't, please. Don't leave me here, please, don't leave me here."

Now she begged and pleaded, stupid bitch, she tried to cling to him but he shook her off like annoying ballast, rain after the storm. What was life worth?

. . .

He pulled away with squealing tires, took off like a rocket, driving for about a hundred yards before hitting the brakes again. The car careened. Me too, he thought, I'll just die too, life is worthless.

But the car stopped. He wouldn't die after all. He jumped out and felt the old familiar trembling rising. He pulled one cigarette after another out of the pack. They broke between his fingers. SHIT, SHIT, *he thought,* you goddamned whore, what have you done to me?!

. . .

He saw the car approaching; its harsh noise grew louder. He saw the girl; somehow she'd managed to get up, limping. Don't put on such an act, he thought, stupid bitch! Just like her mother.

He laughed. What a coincidence; I struck again.

As if she'd heard him, she started to run, into the lights, throwing herself toward them. They picked her up, took her in, and threw her into the air.

But the sky was too high. Too high.

Soundlessly, she fell through the transparent rain.

A high-pitched voice sang in his ears like a memory, and he knew she was dying. He knew she was already dead.

59

He drove home and checked every room in his house. The kids were asleep and his wife, too.

He took a shower, setting the water to seventy degrees. It cooled and calmed him. Then he went into his bedroom, turned the alarm clocks on both sides of the bed back by four hours, pulled the blinds down to shut out the light of dawn, woke his wife, and had sex with her and enjoyed it. He shook his head at himself.

"What time is it?" she asked sleepily as he rolled off her.

"Not that late," he said, holding one of the clocks up to her face. "Here, look."

"You're right," she said. "I could have sworn . . . Where have you been? All of a sudden you were gone."

"I met an old college friend at the party, an uncle of one of the students. We went for a drink," he said. "Just imagine, what a coincidence."

"I see," she said. "Well, it must have been pretty exciting for you to come home in this mood."

She laughed softly and leaned forward to kiss him, but he turned away in disgust.

"Don't," he said, trying hard to suppress the retching.

But she noticed, and ran her hand over his chest. "What's the matter?" she asked. "Are you sick?"

"Yes," he said, jumping out of bed, "I'm suddenly not feeling well. The flu, maybe."

"Maybe you've just had too much to drink," she said. "I can smell it on your breath."

He ignored the reproach in her voice and said, "Yes, could be, go back to sleep," and closed the door.

In the bathroom he vomited, twice, three times, and rinsed out his mouth. He frightened himself when he looked in the mirror. When he went back to the bedroom, she had already gone back to sleep.

He lay awake until morning, until it was time to turn the clocks forward again and pull up the blinds.

60

They walked to the car. It was late, as usual. Dark, even though it was summer. *Amazing,* Franza thought, *where are the days going?*

Felix groaned as they got into the car. His intestines were rebelling, or maybe it was his kidneys, his liver, or his discs, something or other that you schlepp around inside you. He made a face, saw Franza's worried look, and shook his head.

"Are we in a race," she asked, "to see who can get onto Borger's table first?" He gave her a long look and tapped his forehead.

They called Arthur on his cell phone. "We've got him," Franza said.

"Yes," Arthur said, "me too. Reuter."

"Great!" she said. "Excellent! Do you have an eyewitness statement?"

"Of course!" he said, clicking his tongue.

"Great!" she said again. "We'll confront him. Find out his address and call us back. We'll meet there. Good work."

"Roger that," Arthur said, happy about the praise. He called the night-shift team at the police station.

"The address for the following name," he said. "It's urgent." He still felt happy as a little boy, racing through town with flashing lights. It had been one of the reasons he wanted to become a policeman.

61

It was hopeless; he knew it. He couldn't go on like this. His life was slipping away from him. He was OK with that.

. . .

On the evening of the third day he decided not to leave the house or go to work anymore. He passed a concerned-looking Karen and went into the bedroom, locked the door, and lost himself in the photos. He spread them all over the bed, the dresser, the floor, everywhere. He ignored Karen's banging on the door, her demands to sleep in her bed; and he didn't leave the room again until the morning, when the house was empty and quiet.

The children got on his nerves. Karen did, too, with the dark rings around her eyes. He couldn't stand her anymore, couldn't imagine how he'd ever been able to. She didn't know anything about the dark energy pulsing through his veins and driving him mad.

. . .

They were flashing through his mind, Marie, Judith, the child. They were pulsing through his veins.

And him? He wanted to follow the silence.

. . .

And? Nothing else.

62

"He won't be home," Felix predicted grimly as he rang the doorbell. "They're never home. And I always know it in advance. I can feel it in my bones, especially today."

He stretched his back gingerly, waiting for something to crack inside him, but nothing happened.

The door opened within seconds, as if someone had been waiting for the doorbell to ring. On the other side of the door, two young girls looking frightened and silent were huddled up against a woman. Franza immediately thought of Bohrmann's children and wondered what other tragedies this town still had in store for them.

An elderly couple appeared in the background. At least she wasn't alone. At least she'd called in support.

It was past ten o'clock now. The sky was dark, but lamps on posts to the left and right of the door lit up the entranceway to the row house.

The family didn't say anything. They just stared at the detectives.

"Frau Reuter," Franza said and held out her hand, but it wasn't taken. "Do you remember us? We were at your school two days ago."

Karen remained silent.

"We'd like to speak to your husband," Franza said, hating herself for it. How many times had she been the bearer of bad news? How many times had she been the cause of further tragedies, sometimes more damaging than the initial one? All the times she'd brought pain to houses and apartments, again and again, and it never got easier.

There'd been many times she'd wanted to tell Arthur about it, about the pain that gripped her every time and how it held on longer each time. "Look for something else," she wanted to say. "Forget about this job. The pain makes you too lonely. But by the time you notice, it's too late." But she knew she wouldn't tell him any of this, just like no one had told her or Felix. He'd find out for himself, just like they had. It was what it was. They were cut from the same cloth; he didn't have a choice.

"Our son-in-law isn't home," Karen's mother said, stepping up to Karen's side and putting an arm around her. "Who are you and what do you want from him, anyway?"

They presented their IDs. "Police, Homicide Division," Felix said and gave their names. "We're investigating a murder. When do you expect him back?"

"We don't know," the mother said coldly. "It's late. Could you please leave? My daughter's not feeling well, and the children need to go to bed."

Franza and Felix shook their heads simultaneously. *Funny,* thought Arthur, who was standing behind them, *how attuned to one another they are. Like an old married couple.*

"I'm afraid that won't be possible," Felix said slowly. "But please, put the children to bed. May we?" He pushed his way past the mother and into the house. Franza and Arthur followed.

The furnishings were tasteful, some modern furniture mixed with old pieces. Art was hanging on the walls. On the dining table in the middle of the room was a pack of cigarettes. Franza and Felix looked at each other, and he nodded. It was the right brand.

Karen's father began to protest. "Hang on a minute, you can't do that! Just push your way into a house like that!"

"Yes," Felix said. "We can. There's a law for situations like this: exigent circumstances."

Karen spoke. "Was it him?" she asked. "Did he kill her?"

"You should put the children to bed," Franza said and leaned down to the girls, smiling as best as she could.

The grandmother nodded, wiped tears from her face, and took the children out of the room.

"Yes," Felix said, looking at Karen. "We have reason to believe he did."

Karen swallowed. Her lips started to tremble and she sucked them between her teeth. She walked over to a cupboard, pulled out a stack of photos, and threw them on the table. Marie. Photo after photo—only Marie.

"I found them in our bedroom," Karen said, her voice firm and steady now. "He'd locked himself in there yesterday and didn't go to work today. When I got home today he was gone. Only the photos were still here." She fell silent, turned to the window, and looked into the night outside. *Once again,* Franza thought, *looking out the window, into the distance, into freedom, even at night.*

"He kept it to himself," Karen said. "Until yesterday I didn't notice anything, nothing at all. And then you two turned up, and he just snapped. Left the school, took off somewhere, I don't know where. He doesn't talk to me anymore. I can't get through to him anymore."

"Did you know? Were you covering for him?"

She spun around, frightened and angry—a bit of both. "Who do you think I am?"

Felix shrugged. "It wouldn't be the first time."

All is fair in love and war, Arthur thought, and then wondered at what a stupid expression it was.

"His love . . ." Karen said quietly and shook her head. "I don't think it was ever . . ."

She broke off, her face an expression of unhappy yearning. "No, I never had it. Even though I would have done anything for . . ."

Franza looked at Arthur. He was standing perfectly still and listening attentively. She found it touching.

"He's never been happy," Karen said, pulling herself together again. "He was always looking for happiness, but it never came. I don't think he loved me, maybe not even the children. No one. I always had the feeling he was waiting, for someone or something. But it never came, and he was always disappointed. But then, suddenly, there was Marie."

She laughed softly, thinking about it. "It was obvious. He devoured her, right from the start. She took his breath away. Yes, that's how it was, whenever he was around her. He was dying to touch her. I could feel it. His hands would always tremble when she was around. She drove him crazy; I could see it."

She fished a cigarette from the pack, lit it, and opened the window. The smoke curled off into the darkness. She coughed softly.

"Then when she wore that dress on Monday." She turned around, Franza nodded. "He went up to her, whispered something in her ear. They probably arranged a meeting place, so he could . . . Probably . . . everyone saw it. I don't know. I felt ashamed. *Me!*" She shook her head and gave a short laugh. "Isn't that crazy?"

"Do you know where he might be now?" Franza asked and sensed that time was running out. "Think. Do you have any idea?"

Karen shook her head. "No, no idea."

Franza sighed inwardly and closed her eyes for a moment.

"We'll take a look around the house," Felix said.

Karen waved her hand dismissively, taking a deep drag on the cigarette. "Yes, sure, make yourselves at home."

They split up. Felix took the basement and the garage, Arthur the ground floor, and Franza the bathroom and bedrooms upstairs.

She went straight to the bathroom cabinets to look for after-shave. She opened the bottle, closed her eyes, and inhaled the smell. She added coffee and cigarettes and it all fit together. But where was Ben?

Karen came into the bathroom. "I liked her," she said. "You probably won't believe me, but I liked her. You just had to like her. She just had something . . . about her. It was like nothing had been decided yet."

Franza looked up in surprise. She'd heard that before. *Port. I have to ask him,* Franza thought, *yes, I have to. But not today, tomorrow.*

"It's not your fault," she said.

Karen nodded, staring into the mirror. "But it happened any-way." She turned around. "He's got a motorboat," she said. "It's tied up somewhere on the Danube. The key's missing."

Franza looked up as if electrified. "Where?"

"I don't know."

"Think!" She grabbed Karen's arms, squeezing them tightly.

"I really don't know. He never took me along. He said the river was his territory; I had no business there. I was OK with that. I don't like the Danube anyway."

It suddenly clicked in Franza's mind. She let go of Karen's arms and ran out of the bathroom and down the stairs. Things were coming together.

Felix came up from the basement, where he'd found Marie's bag in a wooden box full of old newspapers. But it didn't matter anymore.

"We're leaving," Franza said. "I know where he is. We need Frau Gleichenbach."

63

He couldn't wait to see the fire. It would be a huge blaze—on the water, everywhere. A fireball shooting into the night sky. And he'd be right in the middle of it.

64

The moon was their ally. It was a bright disk in the slightly over-cast sky. It illuminated the Danube and the roads along the shore. They had called for backup: water police, technicians, colleagues who knew the area well, and Robert. They'd also called Judith Gleichenbach. She'd told them to meet her at an inn on the out-skirts of her village. It was near the beach that Franza was con-vinced was at the center of everything they were closing in on.

Judith was already there when they arrived, along with the local officials. Shortly after came the water police by boat, then the technicians carrying enormous searchlights that would bathe the Danube in dazzling light.

Judith Gleichenbach was pale but composed. While the new arrivals were briefed and received their instructions, she stood a little apart, just beyond the light from the inn. The building was situated directly on the river along the road leading through the woods to various swimming spots. The woman who managed the inn with her husband told Franza that the roads weren't used much anymore.

The Danube was usually a very cold river and therefore not particularly inviting, the beaches were stony and not well maintained, and bushes and fallen trees from storms often blocked the way and weren't removed until the fall. The manager could confirm, however, that every now and then boats were tied up at an old dock—rowboats, canoes, and the like. She'd never seen a motorboat there, but then again she hadn't been down that way for a while, three years at least. Why should she? She had her own tidy and well-maintained access to the river.

Had she seen anyone drive past in a Jeep Cherokee that afternoon?

The manager thought about it. She wasn't very good at telling cars, she said, that was her husband's domain. But it was definitely possible that an SUV had driven past that afternoon.

She called to her husband, who'd been waiting quietly behind the curtain at the entrance to the dining room.

"Yes," he said after Franza asked him the same question. He stroked his bald head thoughtfully. "Reuter drove past in his Jeep."

Franza felt a tingling running through her body. So she'd been right. "Reuter. You know him?"

"Yes," he said. "Sure. We went to school together. He's from around here, after all. Why?"

"Tell us," Franza said with an urgency that didn't allow for contradiction or delay. The man raised his eyebrows with surprise, scratched his chin, and thought for a moment. "There isn't much to tell. We weren't friends, just classmates. We lost touch after school. He just disappeared. But a few years ago he turned up again with a little motorboat and asked if he could tie it up at the dock down there."

The landlord pointed downstream. "We got talking, of course. He told me he was teaching at a high school in town, and that he'd studied in America and then stayed there for a few years after he finished. I was impressed. I mean, I've hardly ever been away from here except for one or two vacations in Greece—what's that compared to ten years in New York?"

Franza nodded while keeping one eye on Felix, who was discussing and coordinating the operation with colleagues.

"Well," the man was saying. "On the other hand, there was nothing keeping him here. His parents were dead, no relatives, why stay here?"

Yes, Franza thought, *why stay here?*

"Why do you want to know all this?" the man asked. "What's all the fuss about? Has Reuter done something wrong?"

"No," Franza said, raising her hands reassuringly. An overexcited inn manager was the last thing she needed now. "Don't worry, just a routine matter."

"Routine matter?" He gave her a contemptuous look. "Come off it. I've watched enough crime shows on TV to know that this isn't just routine."

"Whatever," she said, her voice again taking on a tone that allowed no contradiction or delay. "You and your wife need to stay put. I'll be relying on your compliance."

The man's eyes opened wide. "I'll be damned! He must have really done something wrong, old Johannes! Who would have thought?" When Franza had gone, he said to his wife, "She's a tough customer, even tougher than you!" She took a swipe at him, and he laughed.

Felix and Franza took Arthur and Judith Gleichenbach with them and drove through the wood to a small parking area. The Jeep was there. They were the first of the police to arrive.

"Down there," Judith said after they'd gotten out of the car, pointing down a narrow road that wound through the trees for a little bit, and then took a turn and disappeared into the darkness. "That's where the accident happened. That's where she was."

Franza nodded. "Please, come along," she said. "You can tell us later. Where do we go now?"

They put on headlamps and moved forward silently, down a slope, through dense undergrowth and over slippery rocks. Franza was grateful she always kept walking shoes in the car for occasions like this. Finally they saw the Danube shimmering gray through the bushes, and they reached a gravelly beach, which stretched for about twenty yards on either side of them. On their right, close to a large boulder sticking out of the water, was the dock. There were several small wooden boats attached to it.

"Lights out," Felix whispered and everyone complied.

"OK," Franza whispered to Judith. "Thank you very much. Now go back to the car with Arthur and wait for us there."

But Judith shook her head. "No," she said. "I'm staying."

Franza sighed. She realized her authority was worthless in this situation. She nodded. "But keep back."

The motorboat was in the middle of the river. It lay dark and quiet in the water. There were no signs that anyone was aboard. They switched on the floodlights and Felix's voice rang through a megaphone. At that moment the full moon disappeared behind a cloud.

65

So here they are, *he thought and had to smile. Just in time for the show. And what a fuss they'd made.*

He didn't stir, just lay there, looking at the sky, at the moon disappearing behind a cloud. Too bad, *he thought,* no stars to wish me farewell, just a little bit of moon.

So she betrayed me after all, *he thought,* my Judith, finally. *He smiled about this, too.* Oh well, what can you expect? They were all stupid bitches—the whole bunch. Stupid bitches every single one of them. Now it would be over once and for all. To hell with all of them!

He was looking forward to the fire. It would be a huge blaze on the water and everywhere. A fireball shooting into the night. And him . . .

. . . right in the middle . . . in the eye of the storm, in the heart of the volcano.

He could feel the dark energy that had pulsed through him and consumed him as far back as he could remember. Soon it would all be over. It would burst, scatter, and finally land at the gates of hell.

He stood up and turned the key in the ignition. Smiling. Free. Finally.

66

They were taken completely by surprise when the fireball shot into the air. The noise was deafening. The police boat was still far enough away to turn around immediately, and Felix's voice broke midsentence.

A dark figure suddenly had appeared on the boat, and Felix thought he'd raised his hand briefly, like a greeting or a farewell, whichever way one chose to look at it. That's when Felix began his second attempt to get Reuter to surrender. But in the same moment, the boat exploded—from its center, from the body of the person who'd just been standing there.

The fire, hissing and spitting, burned out fast, and within a few minutes it was all over. The Danube was black and calm again.

"Shit!" Felix said from the bottom of his heart, saying out loud what they were all thinking. "Goddamn shit!"

They felt like they had failed because they were too late. They didn't catch him—not in the way murderers should be caught. Instead, they'd fish parts of his body from the river and that was it. He slipped through their fingers and played them to the last. He was always one step ahead, dictating the course of this bitter game right to the end. There would be no interrogation, no questions and no answers.

"It's over," Franza said slowly and put an arm around Judith's shoulders.

"Yes," Judith said. "Over. Really?"

Franza remained silent.

"Let's go," Felix said brusquely. "To hell with it, we're taking off. Robert, you're in charge. Report back to us tomorrow. I'll call the forensic team for you. Fish out what you can and get it onto Borger's table so we can verify it's Reuter. Otherwise we'll have to put out an APB tomorrow, but I don't think . . ."

He broke off, picked up a handful of stones from the beach, and hurled them into the Danube with a shout of rage.

They walked back to the car, Felix leading the way, followed by Arthur, and then Judith and Franza. They left the harsh circles of light from the spotlights and walked up the hill into the darkness.

"Hey!" Felix shouted suddenly, "Stop!" He halted abruptly and shined his flashlight into the dense bushes.

Two darkly dressed figures darted quickly and nimbly through the undergrowth, jumping over roots and rocks like dancing fauns with streaming hair.

"Leave them," Franza said. "We can talk to them tomorrow."

"But wasn't that . . ." Felix began.

"Yes," Franza said. "Cosima and Jenny."

It started to rain.

"Looks like a steady rain is coming," Arthur said, shuddering. "They'll have fun down there! Does anyone know the time?"

They shrugged. "Sometime after midnight."

Then they took the car back to the inn, where the other car was parked and where they'd split up. Arthur and Felix would go straight back to town, but Franza wanted to drive Judith Gleichenbach home.

Arthur's cell phone rang, and he looked at the screen in amazement. "Karolina!" he said, surprised, forgetting for a moment he wasn't alone. "I wonder what she wants?"

"Well, pick it up then you'll find out!" Felix said, slowly getting over his anger. "What do you think she wants? She's lonely without you."

Embarrassed and a little confused, Arthur looked into the rearview mirror. His eyes met Felix's broad grin. Had his unhappy love story really been so obvious to everyone?

"Come on!" Felix encouraged him. "You don't make a woman like Karolina wait, you know."

Arthur picked up and listened for a while. Then his heart began to pound, because Karolina . . . Karolina wanted to make him happy.

She missed his unreliability. It turned out she *could* imagine leading the life of a *shitty policeman's girlfriend* after all. Temporarily at least. Life wouldn't be dull, anyway. Would he come over? She'd ordered sushi.

His stomach lurched, he hated sushi like the plague, but what wouldn't a man do for love. "I'll come right over," he said.

The men drove back to town, and Felix drove while Arthur sat next to him and secretly rejoiced in his luck and cursed Felix for not punching the gas a little harder.

Then Felix had the gall to start a conversation although Arthur was reveling in Karolina-sushi dreams and really had NO time for him right now.

"May I give you some advice? As a fatherly friend, so to speak?"

Arthur sighed and gave a wry smile. *That's all I need,* he thought. He hadn't missed the ironic undertone in Felix's voice. *Shit, sometimes he really gets on my nerves! What's he going to say this time?*

"Of course!" he said. "Anytime."

"Yes, well," Felix said, pausing theatrically. "Between us men. Don't put up with so much. Really, don't let yourself be tossed out like that! That's just going too far. You're a policeman, after all, not some pushover. Our collective reputation is at stake here!"

Arthur stared at Felix, stunned. "Also," Felix continued unperturbed, "all this is going to affect your mental health at some stage. Unless"—he faltered, knitted his brow, and shot a brief glance at Arthur—"are you two into S and M?"

Arthur was speechless. If he was sure of anything, it was that he had not talked about *that incident.* "How," he stammered, "how the hell do you know about that?"

Felix's smile was mild now. "Are we sleuths? Gumshoes? Yes or yes? There you go!"

Arthur swallowed. *Yes,* he thought, *sure, yes or yes.* "And Oberwieser?" he stammered. "Does she know about it . . . ?"

"No," Felix interrupted, patting his leg reassuringly. "Of course not."

Thank God, Arthur thought and tried to unwind a little. *That's the last thing I need!*

"Or if she does . . ." Felix said, "not in any detail, anyway."

He cleared his throat. "Do you want me to go a little faster? Am I driving too slow for you?"

Arthur shook his head. "No, no," he said. "It's all right."

I'll kill you, he thought, *I'll send you straight to the happy hunting ground, and then I'll get mitigating circumstances.*

"Watch it now!" Felix said. "You're not thinking any ugly thoughts, are you?"

Yes, Arthur thought, *that's precisely what I'm doing. The happy hunting ground, Hades, all those things, and with a decent portion of hellfire on top—just like on the Danube a little while ago!*

"Oh, yes," Felix said. "One more thing. In the future, please make sure you get sufficient sleep. You were just unbearable to watch."

OK, Arthur thought, *that's enough.*

He opened his mouth for a long-overdue retort. "And what about yourself? I've got a feeling you'll envy me my nights in a few months' time. I've heard yours are going to be pretty substandard. I'll be happy to tell you about my nights with Karolina then—in all their scintillating colors. Sound good?"

"Ouch!" Felix said appreciatively and sighed. "How malicious!"

67

"Franziska, my dear," Franza's mother used to say in honeyed tones when Franza visited her in the old folks' home in the days just before her death. As always, Franza was annoyed about her full name, which, since childhood, she had considered antiquated and poorly suited to her.

Sometimes she thought about not going, and then the one time when she actually didn't go for her daily half hour—not because of carelessness or laziness, but because her job hadn't permitted it—her mother died.

Of course it hadn't been her fault, the nurses and doctors at the home assured her with surprise. Where did she get that idea? Her mother was an old lady and her heart just couldn't keep up anymore. These things happened all the time.

Franza didn't know what made her think of this now of all times, on the drive back to the village where Judith Gleichenbach lived. Her mother had died two years ago, and Franza was now the owner of the small house where she'd grown up twenty miles downriver. The same house where she'd had to go piggyback as a child when the brook burst its banks and they had to evacuate.

Maybe it was being close to the Danube that caused her to think of all these things, or maybe it was just sheer exhaustion that made her so inappropriately sentimental.

They entered the village, and Judith wanted to get out of the car. "Thank you," she said. "I'd like to walk for a bit."

Franza nodded and pulled over to the side of the road. The village was deserted, and when she checked her watch she saw it was half past one.

"There's one more thing I'd like to know," said Franza.

"Yes?" Judith asked, gazing into the dark village. "What is it?"

"The anonymous caller back then," Franza said. "That was you, wasn't it?"

Judith nodded. "Yes," she said. "Of course. That was me."

She'd already opened the door. There was a chilly breeze, and some raindrops were blowing in. They both shivered.

"Are you sure you won't let me take you home," Franza said. "It's raining."

"No," Judith said, "the fresh air will do me good." But she stayed there, as if waiting for the next question.

OK, Franza thought, *I'll ask it then.* She cleared her throat.

"Why didn't you go to the police? Why didn't you report him? Were you scared of the consequences because you were in the car, too?"

"Scared of the consequences?" Judith thought it over and shook her head. "There wouldn't have been any consequences for me, no legal ones. He forced me back into the car and he beat me like a madman. Any doctor could have confirmed that."

"But," Franza began, "then I don't understand . . ."

Judith closed the door again and thought silently for a moment. The rain was drumming onto the roof of the car, louder now, turning the car into a protective cave.

Hopefully it won't hail, Franza thought while she waited for the answer, looking through the window anxiously at the sky. *If it starts hailing, my car will be ruined.*

"I was pregnant," Judith said.

68

"It was very recent," Judith continued. "I'd only known about it for a few days."

Franza closed her eyes and felt the world falling silent, silent like they were. *The rain,* she thought somewhere in her mind while contemplating the words she'd just heard, the words that were chiseled into the silence like a relief of sadness, a relief of darkness. The rain stopped. *She was pregnant.* It won't hail. *She was expecting a child.*

"Should I have reported him, then?" Judith continued with a desolation and a brokenness in her voice that was overwhelming. Franza knew there'd be no more consolation, nothing. "Should I have? He was the man I loved up until that moment, until everything fell to pieces."

Silence again. No hail.

"Today, yes . . ." she said, "today . . . I know . . ."

She shook her head. "But in hindsight," she said, "in hindsight it's always too late."

She put a hand on Franza's arm. "The burial's on Tuesday," she said. "Will you come?"

It was so quiet, so still, in the car and everywhere. *It can't be,* Franza thought, *not this.* She turned her head slowly, opened her mouth to say something, but had to clear her throat because it had turned dry and sticky.

"No," Judith said. "No. Please don't ask."

Then she got out and started walking down the road. The houses moved closer together, taking her into their circle. She carefully avoided the big puddles on the road.

Franza got out, too, leaned against the car and breathed deeply, trying to suppress the shivering, the tears. There was a fresh smell—how she loved it—in the air and the rain. Tuesday, then. Another Tuesday. "I'll come," she whispered. "Of course I'll come."

The moon was peering out from behind the clouds. A soft sound of singing was wafting through the air from somewhere far away. Clear and high, one single note.

69

Franza startled out of a dream around six o'clock in the morning. Reuter had been sitting opposite her in the interrogation room; the lamp had burnt holes into his eyes, and outside the window, trees were sliding past at high speed.

"I didn't want to kill her," he said, smiling at her. "You have to believe me, Frau Detective."

She was fascinated again by the way the sun caught in his hair, creating sparkling and glimmering spots, which turned into flames. But Reuter didn't burn; he was still smiling at her.

Her eyes flashed coldly back at him. "You mean you didn't want to do it yourself?"

He thought about it for a long time. "Yes," he said eventually. "I guess you could say that."

Trees slid past again, more slowly this time, and she recognized alder trees and willows with their weeping branches blowing in the wind.

"Go to hell!" she said. "Damn you, go to hell!"

He started to laugh. "OK!" he laughed. "If that would make you happy!"

When Port turned up and Reuter started to flirt with him, she awoke and sat straight up in the wide bed. She looked around, confused.

Slowly, her memory returned. She had driven back to town, willing herself not to think anymore, but it hadn't worked. She'd left the autobahn and driven past the theater, past Port's house. The temptation to stop and ring the doorbell, to fall into his bed and into his warmth, had been great, but she hadn't yielded to it.

Suddenly and very conveniently, the Babenberger, one of the few luxury hotels in town, came into view. The prospect of a huge, soft bed and a sparkling clean bathroom had made her pull over immediately and check in.

"You don't have luggage?" the receptionist had asked, eyeing her skeptically.

"No," she answered, putting on her policewoman expression. "Is that a problem?"

"Of course not," he assured her hastily.

"Good," she replied. He needed to get a move on if he didn't want to pick her up off the floor.

The alarmed look on the receptionist's face spoke volumes, and his manicured fingers raced over the keyboard to type all the required information into the computer. Before she knew it, she was checking into an almost indecently large room. She had collapsed on the bed and gone to sleep immediately.

That had been barely four hours ago, and slowly the memories were coming back to her, everything that had happened over the last few days. She got up, wrapped herself in a blanket, and walked to the window. The morning was gray and bleak, as glum as a morning in November even though it was June.

She rested her head against the cold glass and pulled the blanket tighter around her. She hadn't had enough sleep.

A shower, she thought, *my kingdom for a shower!*

She stood in the doorway to the bathroom, looking at the white tiles shimmering in the warm glow of the ceiling lights and the fixtures sparkling like freshly polished pennies, and sighed contentedly.

Good, she thought, *all right, let's face this morning and all that comes next. Ben,* she thought, *where are you, why aren't you calling?*

She took her time in the shower, standing under the stream of warm water with her head tilted back and her hands against the tiles, the water warming her right through and steaming up the bathroom.

I'll order some breakfast, she thought, *bacon and eggs and coffee and croissants and orange marmalade, yes, orange marmalade. Surely they'll have that in a fancy place like this.*

And then, she thought, *I'll try Ben again, and I'll call Max and Port.*

She got out of the shower, put on the bathrobe that was on the shelf next to the shower, fresh smelling and neatly folded, and waited until the steam dissipated and her face was visible in the mirror. Sometimes she could still see the face of the teenager she'd once been, ages ago. Other times it was the face of the twenty-year-old or that of the woman who'd woken up one morning and found that her life was running out unremittingly, toward an end or a beginning depending on how you looked at it. That final face was probably the most normal and at the same time the most bitter fact of her life.

She smiled at herself in the mirror and had to admit she badly needed a haircut. When she realized she was slipping back into the normalcy of everyday life, and that even Marie's death wouldn't change that, tears came to her eyes and she thought of her son and how little she'd been there for him. She wished he were here, and she was filled with sadness for what awaited him.

When her cell phone rang she thought it was him, but it was Port.

"I'm standing by your car," he said. "Where are you?"

She was surprised. "By my car? At this hour? It's the middle of the night for you!"

"Yes," he said, "it is. I'm on my way home. It got a little late. We had the premiere."

"Until now?"

He was a little embarrassed. "No, not until now. So where are you?"

She told him, and he wanted to come up.

When he hugged her, she noticed he was wet and also that he stank of cigarettes, schnapps, and sweat—just what people smelled of after an all-nighter. She liked it.

"You've solved the case," he said. "Haven't you? You seem so . . . serene."

"Yes," she said. "But serene? No."

He saw the bed and staggered toward it.

"Oh!" he said. "I bet it's soft. I bet it's for me." And he dropped onto it and was asleep at once. She shook her head and looked at him. There he was in his T-shirt, shorts, and flip-flops.

You're a crazy man, she thought, shaking her head. *You really are nuts.*

She pulled the flip-flops off his feet and covered him with a blanket. *What do you know about the world,* she thought, *unless it happens onstage?*

But she knew she wasn't being fair. He knew a lot about the world. He knew how to please a woman. He even knew how to please a man with innuendoes. Wasn't that a lot?

She grinned and enjoyed indulging unchecked in her cynicism.

Then she walked to the window and indulged in the time-honored gaze out into the world, into freedom, into boundlessness, into whatever.

It was all doom and gloom outside: wind, rain, and it was not getting any lighter. When the Danube sent the fog, everything sank into a state of insignificance. People wandered around aimlessly as if nothing concerned them.

She walked to the room telephone, ordered breakfast, sent Max a text message saying she'd come home in the afternoon, and went back to bed.

Lauberts came to her mind.

Shit, she thought, *we've got to call off the search. We can't forget that.* His bad conscience had probably made him miss his wife, and he'd gone and joined her in some vacation spot in southern Italy. Right now he was lying in the sun and would never cheat on his wife again. Maybe *she* would be cheating next.

She picked up her phone again, typed *Cancel Lauberts,* and sent the text message to Felix. Then she realized that he'd missed his second appointment with Max. *Frau Brigitte will be pleased,* she typed into her phone, adding five exclamation marks, pushed the "Send" button, and suspected Felix would curse her if he happened to have left his phone somewhere close to his bed. Considering the impossible time of night—or rather morning—they'd all gotten to bed, it was more than likely he'd forgotten to turn it off.

She thought of Brückl and how happy she'd made him by solving the case so fast. There wouldn't be a trial for him to play up to the media, but at least he'd get a few interviews with the local paper.

Then she decided to ask his wife, Sonja, about the strange affinity she'd always seemed to have for square, insignificant men void of any mystery or melancholy. She really wanted to know why.

Franza suspected it had something to do with security and constancy, things Karen Reuter never had.

Kind of crazy, she thought. *Here I am lying in bed in an obscenely expensive hotel, not even five hundred yards away from Port's apartment, and I don't even feel bad.* Was it decadent or just plain stupid? She sighed and thought of the bill waiting for her a few floors below. She definitely could not expense it.

Port stirred and crawled close to her, resting his head against her shoulder. She looked at him, his handsome face and his dark hair. She brushed her hand over his chin, which was prickly like a baby hedgehog. It was how she liked it. It reminded her of Max and of how it was in the beginning, long ago. She thought of the future and wondered what it held for her, and she thought that everyone else was probably right, that one day Port would leave for a bigger and better theater, in a bigger and better city. They wouldn't see each other anymore, wouldn't touch each other anymore, or be there for one another. A small, sad feeling spread inside her, pricking the other, all-encompassing one.

Thank God Port began to snore at that moment, and the pressure that had begun to hold her in its tight grip was released. "Hey," she said, nudging him. "You snore!"

He started, looked at her out of sleepy eyes, and said indignantly, "Not true!" Then he fell back asleep and continued to snore.

She shook him off and got up again. *We'll see,* she thought, *as always, we'll see.*

That had been her mother's mantra. She used to say it at any possible or impossible occasion. For some reason Franza had picked up the habit; maybe it was just a mother-daughter thing.

She had to laugh and wanted to sigh at the same time. Her stomach rumbled loudly, and she hoped breakfast would be there soon. She thought of the orange marmalade and wondered if they had to pick the oranges first. She imagined its bright, sun-like shimmer and the slightly bitter taste, which would melt on her tongue.

She sank deep into the armchair she'd moved next to the bed and pressed her feet gently on Port's behind, to which he replied with a soft grunt. *Just you wait,* she thought and kicked him, once, twice, and then he spun around so suddenly that she gave a surprised laugh. He grabbed her feet and stuck them under his arm, and she felt how tired her bones were, so tired she was sure she'd never get up again, especially not from this armchair, which must have been made for tired bones.

She thought of the case again. Had they forgotten anything, overlooked anything?

As she was drifting off, her cell phone rang. She started. It was probably Max, or maybe Felix wanting to tell her off for waking him.

She looked at the screen and made a sound of surprise.

Ben. It was Ben.

She pushed the "Accept Call" button and noticed her fingers were trembling. "Ben!" she shouted into the phone. "Oh my God, Ben! Finally!"

. . . was a peculiar girl
a peculiar child
now the wind's blown her away
as winds tend to do . . .

marie
in memoriam

ABOUT THE AUTHOR

Award-winning writer Gabi Kreslehner lives and works in her hometown of Ottensheim, Austria, located on the shores of the Danube. There, she is a teacher and is involved in student theater. *Rain Girl* is her first novel for adults and also the first of her books to be translated and published in English.

ABOUT THE TRANSLATOR

 Lee Chadeayne, translator, is a former classical musician and college professor. He was one of the charter members of the American Literary Translators Association (ALTA) and is editor in chief of the ALTA newsletter. Recent translations include Oliver Pötzsch's *The Poisoned Pilgrim: A Hangman's Daughter Tale* and *The Wandering Harlot* by Iny Lorentz.